The Mark

Dr. John Timothy Miller

DEDICATION

To my wife, Francene, daughter, Autumn and her husband, Tim, son, Justin, and his wife Amanda and my five grandchildren Hope, James, Daisy, Everly, and Hannah.

Table of Contents

-

Preface

Sarah awaits trial for refusing to receive the Mark on her forehead or hand, a symbol of absolute allegiance to the New World Order. She faces the possibility of either freedom or death. Sarah had once hoped for a world government that would bring peace and prosperity to the global community. However, after her parents vanished along with millions of others, she discovered that the Christian faith of her family, which she had rejected for years, was true. The Mark serves as a glimpse into the near future where people like Sarah have been manipulated into a global society that transitions from safety and security to destruction and chaos.

The United States, once a great nation, has fallen into this delusion, along with most of the world's governments, as they form the Global World Government (GWG). After only a decade of existence, the GWG suddenly collapses when millions of people throughout the world vanish without warning, causing chaos and anarchy as the global economy crumbles and people start rioting. From this turmoil arises a charismatic leader named Alexander Dimitrov, who claims to have all the answers to the world's problems. Is he a peacemaker or a power-hungry politician who desires to rule the world? Why does he insist that everyone in his newly formed global government receive the Mark on their forehead or hand? You'll have to read and find out.

ACKNOWLEDGMENTS

I wish to recognize a number of individuals who assisted me in the successful completion of this book:

I appreciate Rachel Downie for her excellent editing and typing of this book.

I thank Mitch Green for his patience and excellence in creating the cover page and making suggestions for this book.

I obliged to Pastor Adam Allen for his consultation and ability to prepare my manuscript for publication.

I am grateful to my wife, Francene, for her support, patience and commitment to helping finish writing this book.

I am thankful to my two children, Justin and Autumn, and my five grandchildren for their inspiration and love.

Finally, I am thankful to God for giving me the ability and desire to complete this book for his glory.

Chapter 1

Sarah Rebecca: On Trial for my Life

Help! My name is Sarah Rebecca, and I'm afraid that this is the last time I'll ever be heard from. I'm going to share what is possibly my final testimony about the tyranny of the New World Order to anyone who chooses to listen. Hopefully, some of you still have access to the internet and can comprehend the severity of this letter, as I realize many people have been censored by the New World Order.

With this carefully-worded internet message, I want to give a warning to those who have not yet figured out that the New World Order is not who they claim to be. I can attest to this because I'm currently awaiting my trial, which was ordered by the New World Order Tribunal, for the following indictments:

1. Failure to bow down and worship the Supreme Leader of the New World Order.
2. Non-fulfillment of the order to join the New World Order Council of Religion and believe in the one true Prophet.
3. For proselytizing and participating in the outlawed Christian religion and its false leader, Jesus Christ.
4. For owning and reading the outlawed book called the Bible.

My message to any of my friends who are still alive and have not mysteriously disappeared with millions of others is this: I want to say that I love all of you and hope you receive this message before it's too late. I left the Christian faith that my parents and grandparents taught me to believe and embrace, but I want everyone to know that I have rallied and come back to my God, the Father, and his Son, Jesus Christ.

I wish to tell anyone reading this letter (if you have not already done so) to please repent of any wrongs you have done throughout your life, ask Christ to forgive your sins, and make him the Lord of your life. Please renounce the New World Order and its Supreme Leader, and most importantly, refuse to receive the mark on your forehead or right hand. To receive this mark is to reject God and commit your physical, mental, and spiritual lives to the evil demonic New World Order and its Satanic Supreme Leader.

I believe the Supreme Leader is the Antichrist (The Beast), his Prophet is a false Prophet (The Little Beast), and the mark is the "Mark of the Beast" as predicted in the Bible. In the book of Revelation, the last book of the Bible, the Apostle John warns that anyone who worships the Beast and receives the Mark of the Beast cannot be saved and allowed to go to heaven.

Yes, the New World Order (NWO) is forcing everyone to renounce all world religions, worship the Beast, commit their lives to the New World Order, and prove it by receiving the 'Mark' on their forehead or wrist. Only then can anyone receive NWO protection, food rations, and travel throughout their global empire. But I implore everyone to escape this tyranny while you still can and travel to areas where the NWO is not in control. I have personal knowledge that there are places of refuge found in mountains and forests of the world's continents where the NWO does not control and that resistance forces to NWO have formed. I was once part of one of these resistance groups before I was captured.

"How did I get myself into this mess? How did this happen to the world and country that I once loved? By sharing my testimony, I am sealing my fate as a traitor to the New World Order and will most definitely receive a death sentence. The NWO will find and use this information as written proof that I am guilty of the charges levied against me by the New World Order's Tribunal Council. Do not worry about my probable death, as I have prepared myself to be sacrificed if it will bring any of you to salvation and save you from Hell!

The country I currently live in is one of many countries throughout the globe that joined the New World Order. The country I used to live in was called The United States of America (USA). It is now part of the New World Order (NWO) and has no borders. The former United States was once the country where citizens were free to believe in God as they chose and free to vote and elect their government representatives. This was the nation where people were able to express personal convictions, opinions, views, and beliefs without retaliation from the government or social media watchdogs.

Let me start by giving you a brief history of the United States of America and how it fell to the NWO's tyrannical ways. The United States of America was originally founded on religious freedom when many people from foreign countries found themselves being persecuted for their religious beliefs in their homelands. They fled repressive governments in Europe and other parts of the world whose rulers left them in poverty and dictated to them how and what to believe when it came to God. Groups such as the Pilgrims and Puritans left their home countries of Europe to seek prosperity and religious freedom in the land called America. These brave people willingly risked starvation, storms, and even death to cross the Atlantic Ocean in search of their dreams, to have freedom of religion, make their own destiny, and form their own communities.

Soon after these groups set up colonies in this new world called America and started building a nation, they formed 13 colonies who were originally under British governance. However, for many years, these people found themselves being controlled and overtaxed by Great Britain, which was ruled by King George III. They had no representatives on Great Britain's ruling legislature and felt they had no say in how they were governed. A group of frustrated colony leaders, in conjunction with most of the 13 colony citizens, demanded that King George give them representation on the British Parliament and lower crippling taxes. After numerous attempts to appeal to King George went unanswered, the colonists made the decision to rebel against British rule and decided to form their own government to rule the 13 colonies. They organized the First Continental Congress, whose leaders met in a town called Philadelphia to organize resistance to British governance and to declare their freedom.

These founding fathers of America created "The Constitution of the United States," which was a document that declared liberty for its citizens and the laws, principles, and freedoms they would be governed by. These brave leaders then formed an army of many of the colonists who believed in freedom that would be used to fight the British military and attempt to gain their freedom. This army was called the Continental Army, and the founding fathers selected a man named George Washington, who had military experience fighting for the British during the French and Indian War, as their Commander-in-Chief. After a hard-fought and bloody war, the Continental Army defeated Great Britain, and a new nation was formed called the United States of America."

Under the New World Order, there is no longer a United States of America or a Constitution. All the freedoms that many brave people fought and died for have been extinguished, first by the Global World Government (which I will explain later in this letter), and then more recently by the New World Order.

The government of the United States of America, which was originally based on many Judeo-Christian principles, no longer exists. The freedoms that its citizens enjoyed are all gone, due to the naivety of people like me who, in the wake of the tidal wave of liberal socialism and globalism, steered us towards a one world government. The global government they pushed us towards was originally made up of many once independent sovereign nations, including the United States. We were all fooled as a people and a nation.

I must admit that I was probably the biggest fan of globalism and the socialist philosophy for many years. I believed the lies that our country was inherently racist and had to be remodeled into a global socialist government with greater equality and equity for all citizens. I was led to believe that conservatives were opinionated, naive, and greedy capitalists.

Conservatives believed that the Constitution was an important set of documents that our founding leaders believed its citizens should live by. They believed that the Constitution listed doctrines that the founding fathers determined were to be used to govern the nation, and that these doctrines should not change without extensive scrutiny. On the other hand, liberal socialists like me believed that the Constitution was a flexible document that must change to align with modern-day philosophy and cultural expressions. We believed that the Constitution should be manipulated to bring about the socialist movement doctrines and ideals of the modern world.

Unfortunately, the majority of young people like me believed this socialist philosophy, thinking we were better educated, informed, and had more advanced thinking than the old-fashioned founding fathers.

We believed in more sophisticated philosophies and did not need religion as a crutch. We were adamantly opposed to modern-day conservatives, who seemed to us mostly as Christians who received their information from the outdated Bible. Those old-fashioned zealots like my grandparents, parents, and siblings believed in the principles legislated by the USA Constitution and the Bible, whose truths they believed were given to all people by God.

During my college years, I put my faith in science and evolution rather than belief in God and religion. To me, religion was a false hope of living forever rather than facing the truth that people are going to die, and after that, there is nothing. Also, how can you prove there is a God? Don't get me wrong, I knew my family were believers in this higher power, and they were considered intelligent by most people's standards as they all had earned college degrees. My father, mother, and grandmother graduated from public universities with Bachelor of Science (BS) degrees. My brother had a Master of Business (MBA) degree from a private university. Finally, my grandfather had earned a Doctorate Degree. At that time in my life, I felt that although my family was smart, they had been indoctrinated by archaic ideas and religious fabrication.

Liberal socialist intellectuals such as most of my professors, friends, and I had determined that anyone who did not believe in truth, as we understood the concept, was deceived and should be made to accept our new ideas. We pushed government officials to force conservatives into government "re-education camps" to extinguish their naive ideas, ideals, and beliefs. Our socialist manifesto included:

1. The United States of America was made up of a majority of white racists and privileged citizens who should be shamed for using their power and privilege to repress minorities. Therefore, they need to apologize to Africa and Native Americans for past abuse and pay them reparations.
2. That equity and equality measures should be forced on all businesses, both private and government, through laws made to correct past abuses and injustices.
3. That the government should be legislated by socialist ideas, be global, and have no borders.

Mistakenly, we had embraced these doctrines without ever taking the time to study history, which would have demonstrated that many of our ancestors were opposed to racism and had worked hard to create social change. I learned too late that President Abraham Lincoln, whose followers were conservative Republicans, led the charge against slavery during the Civil War era. His party was supported by abolitionists who demanded that slavery be abolished. Abraham Lincoln and his followers believed that all people of all races and ethnicities were created by God to be equal and that no person should enslave another. Many people during this time were willing to fight and even die for these issues, resulting in thousands of deaths during the Civil War. The Union Northern States patriots, who came from diverse ethnic backgrounds, were willing to sacrifice their lives in order to abolish slavery and give slaves freedom. Most of the slave owners were found in the Southern States and supported the Confederate Army. A group of abolitionists in the Northern States proceeded to smuggle slaves from slave owners in the South to safety and freedom in the North. This was accomplished through a network of transportation routes and safe houses that was called the Underground Railroad. They did this with the understanding that if they were caught smuggling slaves, they could be severely punished or even killed. Unfortunately, I was not taught this in history class or if it was taught, I did not listen. Abraham Lincoln, when he was still President of the United States, was assassinated for his beliefs.

History also showed that President John F. Kennedy, a white Caucasian Democrat, appointed unprecedented numbers of African Americans to high-level positions in his administration, spoke in favor of school desegregation, and strengthened civil rights laws. Attorney General Bobby Kennedy, John's Kennedy's brother, also fought for the enforcement of civil rights laws and for improvements in the employment of African Americans during his tenure. They put into action the brave beliefs of a great leader named Martin Luther King Jr.

Martin Luther King Jr. was an African American Baptist minister who became the most visible leader of the civil rights movement from 1955 until his assassination in 1968. In his "I Have a Dream" speech, he exclaimed that a great American named Abraham Lincoln had signed the Emancipation Proclamation, declaring all men equal. He noted that the architects of our republic and the words of the Constitution promised that all men were guaranteed the unalienable rights of life, liberty, and the pursuit of happiness, both black men and white men. He declared that African Americans were still not free but still under the chains of discrimination. However, he went on to say that despite difficulties, he had a dream for today and tomorrow that all people of all races would not be judged by the color of their skin but by their character. He was later assassinated for his beliefs.

After many years, this country, made up of both political parties, had finally made strides towards freedom for all people of all races and ethnicities. Equality among races was progressively getting better, and many modern-day black and white conservatives wanted equality as much as us liberal socialists. The conservative philosophy was to continue to keep fighting and growing towards a more equitable society by encouraging peaceful protests and working as a society to extinguish racism. The liberal socialist philosophers believed that racism was a major issue in the USA that could only be overcome by forced radical ideology. This racial equality and equity ideology must be achieved by any means necessary, including rioting and looting of cities.

The real problem was that neither the liberal socialists, whom I embraced, nor the conservatives, who my family believed in, would listen to each other's ideas. This led to no consensus and further alienation between the political parties. Also, many of us young people did not truly understand, until it was too late, that many of these modern-day liberal socialists were led by radical anarchists who created and backed dangerous, extreme ideas. They secretly called for the elimination of all family and religious values. We were so intent on changing our country because of past inequities that we lost sight of how far our country had come in becoming more equitable and fairer to the people than any other country in the world. We marched in protest for our cause but failed to look at the websites of certain extreme left-wing organizations that caused our peaceful marches to turn into riots, looting, and hatred for the police. We failed to do our homework and look into the mission statements and horrific goals of these organizations that called for the rejection of Jewish and Christian religious values, the dissolution of traditional families, and for cities to be burned to the ground so that they could be rebuilt as socialist communes, where everyone shared everything equally. However, too late, I found out that these same wicked leaders, who preached these doctrines, were the real haters and racists as verified by their disdain for anyone with religious values, especially Jews and Christians. I realized too late that their real goal was to bring anarchy and the downfall of the United States. The radical socialists wanted the Constitution changed or abolished and remade to meet their demands, rather than realizing that this document had guaranteed the freedoms and rights of its citizens for two hundred years. I realized too late that the socialist agenda was to dissolve the United States government and replace it with a global Marxist one.

I should have known the history of my country, both good and bad, but I was never taught the truth in public school, as my teachers were highly biased toward authors who made up history to match their socialist ideology. I was so caught up in the socialist global government movement that I failed to recognize that the history of countries that had chosen socialism has never worked anywhere in the world. This belief system has always led to power being placed in one authoritative leader from one controlling party. No dissent, even if it is peaceful, is permitted and is soon crushed. For example, the Bolshevik Communist Party, led by Vladimir Lenin, gained prominence when they revolted against the Romanov dynasty that had ruled Russia for centuries as a family of Imperial rule. The Russians, after centuries of totalitarian rule by the Czars and their families, finally rebelled against this type of repressive regime and overthrew them. However, they basically traded it for what they thought would be a utopian government following the ideals of Karl Marx and instead received an even more repressive, authoritative government called communism. In order to achieve the Marxist objectives, normal law-abiding citizens could be sacrificed to make way for this new utopia. Proof of this was demonstrated when their leader, Vladimir Ilyich Ulyanov, who went by the name of Lenin, ordered his secret police to execute as many as 100,000 Russian citizens who did not agree in totality with the communist beliefs. Years later, another Russian dictator named Joseph Stalin became the general secretary of the communist party, and his totalitarian regime proceeded to kill and exile millions of their own citizens, many of them farmers, because they refused to cooperate with forced collectivism. The communist goal was to make everyone equal within a totalitarian regime whereby the government controlled all the jobs, people's rights, and the distribution of all goods and services.

The government officials, instead of serving the people, became their worst enemies, becoming authoritarian and accepting only one-party monopoly of power. This left the common people with no say in the way their government was administered. Eventually, the government controlled everything and took away everyone's freedoms. This government eventually collapsed when the Soviet Union went bankrupt after what was called the Cold War, due to the greed and corruption of communist leaders.

China's history offers another example of a bloody and ruthless takeover by socialists (communists). The movement was led by Chairman Mao Zedong, who gained complete authoritarian power and decided to purge all people that disagreed with his socialist policies. He proceeded to murder millions of Chinese, many of whom were already communists, who he saw as threats to his power-hungry authority. The aftermath of his rule forced the majority of the Chinese population to live in subservience to the socialist dictatorship government.

Nazi Germany provides yet another lesson on failed socialist governments, led by a charismatic yet evil dictator named Adolf Hitler. He convinced the German people to believe the Nazi party's radical socialist ideology, which led to the death and subjugation of many citizens. He led the German nation into a world war in which millions of innocent people died. In order to stifle any dissent to his policies, Hitler created secret police called the Gestapo, who killed thousands of German citizens who disagreed with the policies of the Nazi party. To ensure that the people of Germany would not rebel and try to overthrow the Nazi party, Hitler and his authoritarian government made a law requiring all German citizens to register their guns. Nobody thought that this was a major issue as it would allow the police to find criminals who used guns in committing crimes faster. However, once everyone's guns were registered with the government, the Gestapo came and confiscated all the citizens' guns. This way, no citizen had any means to fight back against an evil dictator and his hand-selected government officials. Hitler's disdain and hatred for Jews, political dissidents, the mentally handicapped, and certain ethnic minorities in Germany led to the murder of millions of innocent people in World War II.

Chapter 2

The Fall of the United States of America

How did people fail to notice the creeping ideology of liberal socialist globalism in the United States? Why didn't I heed the warnings of my parents, brother, sister, and grandparents, who cautioned that a worldwide government would have catastrophic consequences? My grandfather, whom I called Pops, once said, "Sarah, the Bible warns us that in the end times, a worldwide government will be taken over by a wicked ruler filled with the devil himself. He will come in the name of peace, but the Bible says there will be no peace. He will hail from a country that is not a major power, and no one will be prepared for his global takeover. His heart is evil, and he seeks power and authority over the world, including the United States of America. He will try to force you to take his 'Mark.'"

To which I responded, "Pops, I don't believe in the Bible, as it is filled with fairy tales. We must create a new world free of religious bigotry." Sadly, Pops, along with my grandmother, father, mother, and siblings, has disappeared without warning or explanation, along with all the other Christians around the world. I now realize that this disappearance is what the Bible calls the rapture, and I wish I could find Pops now and tell him he was right.

Anyway, getting back to my story of how this great country fell into madness. It all started when a few multinational corporations began buying up the majority of communication networks in the United States. They gained control of radio, television, social media, and news networks, all with the permission of government officials who were paid huge sums of money as payoffs to not enforce antitrust laws that would prevent any corporation from monopolizing any industry. This lack of enforcement allowed a few mega-corporations to monopolize all communication networks in the USA, giving them access to spy on private citizens' information, including their phones, computers, televisions, and home social networks.

These mega-corporate leaders, in cooperation with their paid-for corrupt government officials, used the power and influence of the wealthiest country in the world, the USA, to force other countries to purchase their corporate products. Soon, most countries in the free world were being manipulated by the same wealthy corporate owners. These billion-dollar companies originally contributed immense amounts of money to politicians in the United States through paid lobbyists, who used the money to manipulate government officials into allowing censorship of anyone who disagreed with socialist thoughts or issues. The corporate leaders' motives for forming a global government were based on their desire for more profits to be made from expanding into other countries. They disregarded the freedom that the United States of America provided them to create their corporations in the first place and wanted to become multinational corporations. They proved their hypocrisy by opening up new emerging markets in authoritarian governments such as China, Russia, Pakistan, Saudi Arabia, and Venezuela, which had a history of oppressing their citizens, especially women and minorities. However, because of their lust for making huge amounts of profits, these corporate globalists continued to overlook human rights abuses, such as using underage children as labor, paying barely affordable wages, placing citizens in internment camps because of their ethnic backgrounds, and forcing people to work unbearable hours.

Soon, all major news networks were owned and operated by a few corporate socialist globalists who, in turn, pressured their employees to adopt a socialist agenda. The only disagreement towards creating a socialist world government in the USA was coming from conservative networks of radio and cable television news networks. These conservative communication networks were eventually forced off the airwaves by liberal socialist-controlled government officials who made policies and laws against any anti-government rhetoric.

Next, the corporate owners manipulated their paid politicians to pass a law requiring all guns in every American household to be registered, under the pretense that this would aid in finding and prosecuting criminals who used guns to commit crimes. Once this law was passed by a liberal socialist-controlled House of Representatives, Senate, and President, and the uproar from gun owners had subsided, the government passed another law making all guns illegal, despite it being against the Second Amendment of the United States Constitution that granted citizens the right to bear arms. Finally, similar to the historic actions of the German Nazi party, the federal government dispatched the military to confiscate the guns of all registered gun owners in the USA, effectively preventing the people from having the means to fight against a totalitarian government.

As these corporate and government officials gained more power, they refused to listen to the needs and wants of the people and used the government to force the masses into doing what they believed was right. The government socialist elite believed that they were more intelligent and informed than the common people, and thus knew what was best for them.

What many people, including myself, did not understand was that there existed a secretive group of "Deep State" leaders who had taken control of the majority of government officials and leaders of multinational corporations. These members, including powerful former government officials, corporation owners, and rich elitists, had a goal of ruling over a world government led by their hand-picked leadership team, which would enact their goals through a new modern global constitution with corresponding laws. They kept their global agenda a secret for many years by communicating over the deep web and waited for the opportunity to enact their global agenda.

After gaining control over the media, television, radio, and social networks, the deep state corporate liberal socialists controlled all information that was disseminated to the citizens of America. They slowly convinced everyone that a one-world socialist government was in their best interest. By confiscating the guns of law-abiding citizens, they no longer had to worry about the people rebelling against the direction the country was going. Furthermore, by manipulating voter election laws, they ensured their socialist agenda and one-world government would be enacted, as only one party had power over all branches of the United States government.

If only young liberal progressive leaders, like myself, had understood that we were being manipulated by evil deep state corporate globalists with an agenda of controlling us through lies and deceit. If only we had listened to the lessons of history, which demonstrated that authoritarian socialist regimes had completely controlled their citizens through manipulation, censorship, eliminating basic human rights, and controlling the information that people received from a government-run press.

However, the question remains, how did this happen in the United States of America, where its Constitution guaranteed basic human rights and freedom? The answer is that liberal socialists like myself were misled to believe that conservatives were stupid, racist, haters, and religious zealots. Instead, we liberal socialists were deceived into believing that we could create a one-world government with a better constitution than the original USA Constitution, which had guaranteed our freedom our whole lives. Unfortunately, we were wrong.

Chapter 3

The Global World Government is Formed

Once again, the United States of America and other countries are slowly collapsing due to corrupt elected officials who are being paid off by deep-state corporate lobbyists. These lobbyists have convinced many of us that a one-world government is necessary. However, the deep-state corporate leaders who bought and controlled these government officials would be the ones in charge of the world's financial markets, manipulating the population towards this new and profitable global society.

The deep-state plans came together after they funded a project that exposed the world's population to a new type of germ warfare called a viral plague. By mutating a killer virus that attacks vulnerable populations, such as senior citizens and those with weakened immune systems, and releasing it worldwide, they were able to create panic and get rid of a no longer productive societal group. The deep-state believed that senior citizens, for the most part, were conservative, patriotic, and needed to be eliminated. Their rationale was that the world was already overpopulated and decreasing the numbers was crucial to their global plan. Although some of the deep-state leaders were seniors, they were to be spared with a pre-planned antidote as they were deemed important people.

This happened after years of secretly placing like-minded liberal socialist teachers and administrators in public-school systems and universities, where they taught their students that socialistic globalism was in everyone's best interest. Parents were not consulted, as the elite teachers knew better than parents what was right for their children.

Before the pandemic, senior citizens were among the most vocal opponents of socialism and global government, warning Americans that embracing a one-world government would mean sacrificing the freedoms that World War I and World War II veterans fought hard to preserve. These seniors, along with other conservatives of various ages, constituted about half of the country's population. However, the liberal socialist globalists managed to eliminate the senior opposition to socialistic global government when millions of seniors died from a premeditated viral plague. As a result, the conservatives were now outnumbered and outvoted when it came time to decide whether the USA should remain the same or help form a new global government.

With the deep state-funded liberal socialist government officials now controlling the majority of its citizens, they could proceed with their plans to establish a new global government. They exerted political pressure on other countries to join them, arguing that by giving up their autonomy and forming a world government, they would enable the countries to be part of a great global empire that would share the wealth of the United States of

America. The United Nations provided the initial structure, but most of the countries that already belonged to it (which had little real authority over the sovereign nations that made up its core) voted to reorganize it, make it the world governing body with strict laws and rules, and rename it the "Global World Government (GWG)." To make this happen, the United States government brokered deals between the powerful corporate leaders and most of the world's political leaders to join the Global World Government. This new world governing body would include most of the planet's countries from Europe, Asia, Africa, South America, and North America, except for China, Iran, Russia, and Israel.

The GWG leadership was to be elected by representatives from former nations. However, the deep state paid bribes to these representatives to ensure that their hand-selected leader, Thomas Carter, was made Chancellor. He personally selected his own cabinet, which was also approved by the deep state leadership. The deep state leadership group was comprised of the world's most influential, powerful, and wealthy corporate leaders who believed they were the only ones intelligent enough to create a society where they could make all the subordinate people believe they were free and equal, while still controlling them by placing them in subsidized communal housing, industrial, and farming communities. The elite leaders would continue to live in luxury, while the common people were not responsible or smart enough to make the right decisions for themselves or others and needed to be governed, controlled, and monitored. To the deep state elite, most people were like sheep who needed to be manipulated and herded into submission. Only they, with superior intellects, could lead the citizens of the world into new paths of equity and equality. They had been planning this world government for many years and finally had the opportunity they were waiting for. They manipulated this global power takeover by convincing the people of the world that the threat of global warming and its catastrophic effects on nature and humans could only be solved by a global government. Eventually, the goal was to also take over China, Russia, Iran, and Israel by creating a worldwide currency and restricting trade to these countries. This manufactured global Utopia government would meet all the deep state's missions and goals.

Chapter 4

The Disappearance of Millions

The Global World Government (GWG) lasted for ten years until it suddenly collapsed without warning. The loss of millions of tax-paying citizens who disappeared in a single day could not have been predicted. All the plans for world domination by the Deep State and the GWG were destroyed when people from around the world vanished without explanation. Pilots flying airplanes and drivers of trucks and cars disappeared, causing crashes on highways and train derailments, explosions, and thousands of deaths and displaced people. Mass hysteria erupted as the loss of life mounted. The GWG soon went bankrupt as the loss of so many tax-paying citizens caused global markets to collapse. China, having spent billions on building and maintaining power grids for the GWG, shut down all power to its citizens. Additionally, a cyber war between the major world powers destroyed the GWG's communication systems.

As the world's power grids shut down and computer-operated systems were destroyed, people had no electricity to heat

23

or cool their homes, communication networks went dark, and riots broke out in the streets. The World Bank and the World Stock Exchange collapsed as people began withdrawing their money from banks and demanding cash. The heavily leveraged GWG banks could not possibly give the people their money back, and they began to close, much like the depression of 1929-1941. Chaos and pandemonium swept across China, Russia, Iran, and Israel, who were still tied into the world banking system, as their money disappeared.

Many theories emerged as to how and why so many people disappeared at once. Some believed it was caused by alien abduction, others by Jihad terrorists, and still others thought it was a conspiracy by China and Russia to gain control of the planet. However, the disappearances were actually the Rapture, a phenomenon that my parents, grandparents, and Sunday School teachers had warned me about. My grandmother had often said, "Sarah, please commit your life to Christ now before it is too late. If you wait and the Rapture comes and you're not saved, you will be left behind." The Rapture, according to my grandmother, was when believers in Jesus Christ would suddenly disappear and be taken up to be with Christ in the air and ushered into heaven. Those left on earth would soon face God's wrath on the rebellious people of the world who hate God and people of faith. This ushered in the Tribulation, a time when the Antichrist (the Beast) and an evil religious leader (the Little Beast) would take over the world and crush all rebellions throughout the planet. The Antichrist would arise from one of ten nations that were originally part of the Old Roman Empire.

At the time, I thought the warnings about the Rapture and the end of the world were hogwash and ignored them. My religious values had been stolen from me by liberal socialist atheists who had convinced me that science was the only god. However, the rise to power of the Antichrist was happening before my eyes as a world leader had been preparing for years for a global takeover. The greed of major corporations and their puppet deep state global government officials was exposed when the global markets crashed due to the disappearance of millions of people. The collapse of the GWG was swift, as were the independent countries of Russia, China, and Iran. Mass worldwide confusion and anarchy ensued.

Chapter 5

The New World Order Rises

A genius and corrupt corporate entrepreneur, aided by his national government and a global corporation called Hexigon, had been gradually purchasing the power grids and communication networks of many nations throughout the world for years. He had quietly built up his military and stockpiled nonperishable food supplies, enabling him to manipulate the chaos caused by the disappearance of millions of people and eventually gain control over the power grids, electronics, and communication systems of the world. His name was Alexander Dimitrov, and he was known as a "Charismatic Leader." He was able to quickly and efficiently restore the communications and power grid of his own country, Moldovia, which was considered by most of the global community to be a small and inconsequential nation.

Once Moldovia was running smoothly again, Alexander prepared to make an offer to ten former European countries, previously governed by the Global World Government, to join him in his New World Order (NWO) government. However, three of these countries refused to consider his proposal, believing that Alexander was not someone to be trusted. This enraged Alexander, who had built a massive military machine consisting of advanced weapon systems and a 500,000-person army, in preparation for the world collapse. On his orders, his generals quickly and efficiently stormed into these three countries, taking control of their governments and citizens in blitzkrieg fashion.

After using his military might to make an example of these three countries, Alexander convinced six other former European and Global World Government countries to take his offer seriously. These six countries were frightened and did not want to go to war, so they soon capitulated and voluntarily joined this New World Order. Alexander promised them that their power grids and communication systems would be quickly restored, saying, "I will give you peace and prosperity like you have never seen! I have the way to eternal security and hope for greatness! I promise you peace in exchange for your loyalty and trust in joining my New World Order government."

Rumors about Alexander spread throughout the revived European network, with some claiming he was a master manipulator, others thought he was an insane madman hungry only for power and fame, while others called him a great leader or even the Messiah. Regardless, he was so charismatic and successful that the citizens of this newly formed global government declared him their Supreme Leader. Alexander, who now controlled ten countries, including Moldovia, proceeded to orchestrate alliances with all the major countries of the world, including what was left of the Global World Government. These countries gave up their claims to government independence and fell under the New World Order in exchange for the NWO restoring power grids, communications, and providing food.

This was easy for him as the leadership of the now collapsed GWG were no longer a threat to his dictatorship. Many of the original deep state leadership committed suicide when their dream of a one world government, with them in power, was gone. The deep state corporate leaders and their politicians had either committed suicide, as they were financially bankrupt, or they were murdered by investors who had lost all their money to these notorious globalists. As a result of the collapse of the Global World Government, most countries soon followed suit. The promises made by Alexander Dimitrov seemed reasonable to the leaders of the old GWG countries who were in complete disarray and desperately needed food, communication, and electricity restored - all of which Alexander had promised to deliver. In addition, by joining the New World Order, the remaining leaders would be guaranteed a seat in the new legislative body, and Alexander personally promised stability and order. Agreements and alliances were made, and most countries sold their national sovereignty by pledging allegiance to the New World Order. Because of his instrumental role in bringing about this global transformation, Alexander was nominated and humbly accepted the title of Supreme Leader. Nearly all countries in the world were now united under this New World Order Government. Alexander, as the Supreme Leader, promised to bring all religions under the authority of one religion, with major religious leaders having a seat on the new One World Religion Council. The Muslims, Hindus, Buddhists, Unitarians, and many other religious groups each selected their most prominent leader to join the council, which was led by Abaddon, the prophet of the New World Order. The only groups denied a seat on the Religion Council were the Jews, who were widely hated, and the mostly extinct Christians who had mysteriously vanished. The nation of Israel refused to join the New World Order and thus retained their sovereignty. China and Russia, which had been thrown into chaos and rioting by the disappearance of millions of their citizens, were so large and disorganized that they had no ruling government and were considered insignificant and non-threatening to the New World Order.

Most of the corrupt politicians in various nations had sold out their countries to Alexander in exchange for wealth, a tradeoff that many had accepted from corporations in the past. Consequently, their countries became part of a new global system of government. The prospect of restoring power to heat homes and use social media would be used to persuade the remaining people to accept this new order. Alexander Dimitrov guaranteed equal power to leaders in running the new world government, and all citizens of the world were promised equity and equality regardless of their race, ethnicity, sex, or sexual orientation. All world leaders saw merit in this proposal, believing they had superior intellect compared to their common citizens. This New World Order was designed to protect the leaders' personal financial interests, and another advantage of joining it was the potential to end religious fighting and wars by having all religions under one ruling council. Alexander thought to himself, "I am the greatest leader the world has ever witnessed. I am the only person who has ever lived that can govern the entire planet!"

Despite this promising vision, Alexander knew that Israel would be a roadblock to his plans of world domination as it refused to join any global government. Israel's leadership claimed that after being denied nation status for many years by the rest of the world, they intended to govern themselves now that they were finally a nation again (after World War II in 1948). Furthermore, Israel had not suffered as much as other countries during the disappearance of millions, and their infrastructure remained intact after the cyber wars. As a result, Alexander determined that the best way to deal with Israel was to sign a peace treaty with them until he could find a way to destroy this arrogant nation and its people.

Chapter 6

Sarah- My Life Story

Returning to my story, I, Sarah Rebecca, feel compelled to describe the events leading up to my imprisonment and my impending trial, which could result in either life imprisonment or death. Allow me to begin with my life story. As a young girl of four years, I was carefree and playful, often teasing my siblings and grandparents, whom I loved deeply. My grandfather, fondly known as "Pops," would read me Bible stories and let me play with his Lionel trains. My grandmother, "Granny," would teach us how to bake and sew and treat me as if I were the most important child in the world. My parents, Rebecca and Jacob, were wonderful, always taking us kids to the park, teaching us to swim, taking us to Sunday School, and making us feel loved.

My older sister, Faith, was always looking out for me, ensuring that I did not get into trouble or harm myself. My brother, Joshua, or "Josh," was the middle child, and he would let me pretend to be stronger than him and "beat him up." But in reality, he could have easily defeated me. These happy times continued until I began attending public elementary school, where I encountered some very strange teachers who confused and terrorized me. One teacher, whom I will refer to as Ms. Bret, wanted me to decide whether I was a boy or a girl. I staunchly declared that I was a girl and would always be a girl, and that God had made me a female. My parents had taught me to embrace my gender and that God had created me as a beautiful girl.

In sixth grade, I developed a crush on a boy named Dustin and was thrilled when he asked me to the school dance. However, we soon went to different junior high schools, and my interest in him waned. Despite these changes, I remained a believer in God and frequently prayed to Him for guidance and help, which He always provided.

In junior high school, my health teacher, Ms. Jones, informed us that individuals could choose different sexual orientations. She had undergone a sex change and was now a woman. I respected my teachers and treated her no differently despite her drastic change. She explained to the class that science offered many choices for one's sexuality, including being transgender, transvestite, gay, lesbian, transexual, or other gender identities. However, I remained steadfast in my Christian faith and continued to believe that God created us as male or female.

During high school, I enrolled in courses that my parents would have disapproved of, such as Evolution, Gender-Neutral Writing, Diversity and Inclusion, African American Studies, and US History Lies and Propaganda. I found these courses to be intriguing and believed that they were necessary to bring about radical cultural changes, which my teachers advocated for.

However, these teachers subtly altered my beliefs about my country and my faith, shifting me away from patriotism and belief in God and toward acceptance of evolution and atheism and the notion that our country was hateful and racially divided.

Another issue that I frequently faced in high school was bullying. Many kids liked to pick on others, and I was not an exception. During my freshman year, I was smaller and weaker than some of the other girls and was pushed around a lot. However, after a year of being bullied and participating in sports that made me stronger and faster than most kids my age, I decided to fight back. From my sophomore year onwards, I stood up not only for myself but also for my friends and other abused classmates. I was always the one who stepped in and defended the weaker kids who were being bullied. As a result, I had to go to the principal's office on several occasions. Although my mother was disappointed in my behavior, my dad and grandpa were proud of me for standing up to bullies, as they had always taught me to do. I am still proud that I stood up for those who were being hurt or abused, both on the cyber network and in real life, as this has shaped my character to this day.

I was very good at all sports, but basketball and softball were my favorites. I loved playing basketball and softball in gym class and soon joined an AAU women's basketball team, where I competed often. I had initially played softball but lost interest in it as it seemed too slow. Basketball had become my addiction.

Senior high was filled with tremendous pressures coming from a variety of sources including teachers, boys, girls, transgenders, straits, gays, lesbians, jocks, Christians, etc. Every group was trying to influence me to be like them. I was always an independent nonconformist and I chose my own paths and friends. Most of my friends told me I was good looking even though at times I felt like a dork. I had a pretty face with naturally blond hair which the younger boys liked. I was not yet attracting the older boys in 9th and 10th grades as my breasts were small, probably because I was an athlete and had a low percentage of body fat, thus causing me to be a late bloomer in the breast department. My breasts gradually caught up with the rest of my body and I started attracting upperclassmen and even some college students when I was in eleventh and twelfth grades. I was taught in Sunday school and by my parents to dress modestly, as they believed it would discourage boys from lusting after me. My Granny took it a step further, advising me to wait until marriage before having sex. According to her, this would make the experience special for my future husband, and God would be pleased. Despite this, it was becoming increasingly difficult to maintain my virginity, especially with all my friends viewing it as a rite of passage for late high school girls, particularly when it came to prom.

In the eleventh grade, I fell in love with Jimmy, who reciprocated my feelings and expressed his desire to marry me. As a senior, Jimmy was an attractive, athletic individual with a great build. He was also the starting halfback on our high school football team, which I enjoyed watching. We shared many interests, especially in sports. Until this point, I had held onto my virginity as a way of staying true to my Christian beliefs, which advocated waiting until marriage before having sex. However, after Jimmy asked me to prom and expressed his love for me on multiple occasions, I realized I loved him too. I made the decision that I would have sex with him the night of the prom.

This all started when Jimmy and I left the prom early and went to a hotel, where we had sex. My girlfriends had all been sexually active for years and encouraged me to follow suit. They believed that if something felt good, you should do it. As a result, I succumbed to peer pressure and went against my Christian beliefs. Since it was my first time, the experience was painful and dissatisfying. Jimmy and I continued to have sex regularly, but he eventually dumped me without warning. He wanted to date other people since he was going to college in the fall. I'm grateful that I didn't get pregnant because I insisted on him wearing protection.

As I entered my senior year of high school, I started to drift away from God. I wanted to make my own decisions and choices, separate from my parents. My friends were all experimenting with drugs and alcohol, and I found myself following suit. I started smoking marijuana and drinking alcohol, and while I never tried any hallucinogenic or harder drugs, I knew I needed to be careful.

I chose to stick to smoking marijuana and drinking alcohol, as they were my preferred substances. While some of my friends experimented with hallucinogens and cocaine, I had a personal code to only get a buzz on alcohol or pot without losing control. However, I loathed not being able to make sound judgments, even though I occasionally got drunk and stoned to the point of not remembering what happened the previous night. I made a promise to myself to never let that happen again.

My closest friend Samantha always urged me to "live life to the fullest right now, because tomorrow we might die." I replied that it scared me because my grandfather, Pops, had warned me about a Bible verse: "For the wages of sin is death but the gift of God was eternal life." He also explained that someday, we would have to "go before the throne of God and answer for the wrongs (sins) we committed in our life." Nevertheless, he emphasized that "if I accepted Jesus Christ as Lord and Savior, my sins would be forgiven, and God would only judge me on the good things I did with my life and for his kingdom."

At the time, I valued my friends' opinions over the advice given to me by my parents and grandparents. Although I knew I would give my life to Christ eventually, I felt I wasn't sinning as severely as other kids my age, so I decided to enjoy life to the fullest. However, little did I know that there would be serious consequences to my choices. Gradually, I was drifting away from my upbringing, especially my Christian faith.

The next thing I knew, I was enrolled in a prestigious private liberal arts university. My parents had hoped I would attend a Bible-believing Christian university, but that didn't fit my plans at the time. I believed in God and wanted a good education, as well as to find a husband. This choice, however, proved to be a costly mistake, as my faith in God and people would soon be severely tested.

As an intelligent, pretty, and athletic young woman, I quickly became a starter for the university's basketball team. With a newfound confidence in my appearance, I was feeling on top of the world. Soon, I found myself in a coed dorm with separate men's and women's halls. Although my father cautioned me that young men in college were often only interested in sex and would soon lose interest in me, I didn't tell him that this had already happened to me in high school with my first love, Jimmy. My mother simply cried and said she would miss me.

Campus life quickly consumed me, and I joined a sorority, made friends in the dorms, and did well in school. My sisters in the sorority became close friends, and we discussed boys, parties, and school events at length. However, basketball felt more like work than fun, and I eventually told the coach I was quitting. He wasn't pleased, but agreed that if I wasn't willing to give 100% to the program, then I should quit.

My friends and I were more interested in going to football games, parties, and playing on social media than we were of what was happening in the real world. Little did we know that powers and principalities from fallen angels were influencing the minds of government employees, past presidents, corporate leaders, and lobbyists to plan the downfall of the United States and a move toward a one-world socialist government, where elitists would rule. Despite our lack of knowledge, we took for granted the guarantees of free speech, freedom of the press, religious freedom, and the guarantees of life, liberty, and the pursuit of happiness outlined in the Constitution of the United States. This lack of understanding made us impervious to what it meant for our ancestors and war heroes who died for this country's freedom and for the flag. We grew up with great freedom and felt it would last forever.

The vast majority of professors were liberal socialists who preached their radical ideology, claiming that capitalism was wrong, and that our country was racist in its history. They believed that we needed to redistribute wealth from those who had been successful financially to those who were poor and had not been given the same opportunities. Although this bothered me somewhat, I was taught by both of my grandfathers and my father that if you wanted to succeed in life, you had to work hard in school, work, and life.

My grandfather Robert had built a successful business from scratch, together with his wife my grandma Darcy, which took many hours of hard work and effort. My other grandfather, Pops, spent over 10 years in college learning as much as he could to become a professor, administrator, and nationally recognized coach at a major university. Pops had a comfortable living, but he told me that he gave up many opportunities to make a lot of money in business for the more intrinsic rewards found in education, such as helping students meet their life goals and careers. He believed strongly that God had placed him in higher education to give students a conservative view of the world. He explained that our country was successful because conservative democratic principles made us the best nation in the world. We have a strong constitution that, when strictly adhered to, guarantees many freedoms that other countries deny.

Conservatives believe that our country provides the best opportunities for all individuals, regardless of race or ethnicity, to obtain good jobs, establish businesses, and achieve their lifelong objectives. Pops explained that the majority of university professors across the country were liberal and advocated for a socialist society in which the government controls all aspects of people's lives. In Pop's view, this is not true freedom but rather authoritarian manipulation. Although socialism may sound appealing at first glance, history has shown that it has never succeeded anywhere in the world.

Despite my upbringing, I found myself gradually embracing the left-wing ideology that the majority of my professors expounded, including the redistribution of wealth from those who had money to those who did not. They also preached that the United States was a white-dominated society that was systematically racist toward black people, and that our country's leadership originally bought and sold slaves during the early founding of our nation, while never allowing African Americans to enjoy the same privileges as whites. It was on their backs that America became great. Therefore, I believed that African Americans deserved reparations from white people in America, even though I was white myself. I always tried to help the underprivileged and women who had been bullied, so I now made giving reparations to black people a major part of my ideology.

I was also persuaded, through strong indoctrination, to believe that God did not exist. My science professors claimed that anyone of high intelligence with multiple degrees, like themselves, could see that we evolved through millions of years of evolutionary processes. They asserted that this was a scientifically proven fact, and that we could not possibly prove God's existence, as this was speculative and could not be verified by their proven methods of scientific inquiry.

Finally, the majority of my professors were proud of their left-wing ideological beliefs. They had convinced me that women had the right to abort their unborn child at any time during pregnancy. They claimed that another advantage of abortion was that it helped prevent overpopulation. These professors also bragged that the Supreme Court had originally decided that women had this right, so I believed this lie like so many others. Later, the Supreme Court decided that this was not a constitutional right, and that the people of each state should be allowed to vote on whether abortions were legal. This made these professors livid, and they constantly screamed against people who believed that unborn children had the right to live. These same professors were convinced that the United States was relatively evil because capitalism was depleting the earth's finite resources, and their expansionism was wrong and needed to be stopped. According to the left-wing ideology, there should be no government borders, and only one global society, whereby everyone shares its resources. This was the best method to ensure that all the world's goods and services were evenly distributed, that racial equity and equality could be strictly enforced, and the environment could be saved through strict laws that only a one-world government could mandate. I believed these lies for a long time because I felt that with all their wisdom and knowledge, these professors were the enlightened ones. They knew the path to creating a utopian world where everyone could share the work and resources, and commune together in an enlightened, race-free environment. In this utopian society, everyone was equal and prosperous. This was only possible if we were to throw out our parents' archaic religions, gods, and family values. We could all be citizens of a new global society that we could create. They encouraged us to divorce ourselves from our parents and families and become brothers and sisters of the world!

Looking back on my life, as I face certain death at the hands of the New World Order government, I realize that we were all being manipulated by demonic forces that had entered into the hearts and minds of evil people to destroy us all. I finally understand that I should have stuck with my original belief in an all-powerful God and His Son, Jesus Christ, who loved me and wanted what was best for me. I should have believed my parents, siblings, and grandparents, who believed in God, instead of taking the belief system of my so-called friends and most of my college professors, who believed that humans could be their own gods, making their own decisions on what is good and evil. They believed that through socialism, people could create a utopian one world government.

Chapter 7

My only Conservative Professor

One college professor, Dr. John Timothy, told me the truth, but my stubbornness and indoctrination by my grand utopian ideas prevented me from believing him or my parents. In his class, he presented the conservative view that government is accountable to the people and that its primary purpose is to provide services and protection. He talked about the principles on which America was founded, including Judeo-Christian values, strict adherence to the Constitution, and the protection of rights such as freedom of speech, religion, and the press, as well as the right to bear arms to safeguard citizens against government tyranny. Unlike other professors, he actually cared about our life experiences both in and out of the classroom.

When I went on a college outdoor club trip to the Florida Keys with Dr. Timothy, I found out that he was also a successful coach who had led his teams to several national championships. He was different from other university professors and administrators, genuinely caring about us and helping to break down the wall between faculty and students. This was achieved when Dr. Timothy and a group of twelve students traveled to Florida in a 15-passenger van. On the way, we shared stories of our lives, boyfriends, girlfriends, career goals, and good and bad experiences.

The trip took us 20 hours to drive to Miami, where we boarded a boat and sailed to the Bahamas.

The purpose of the trip, according to Dr. Timothy, was to "turn us on to the magnificent beauty and challenges of exploring the great outdoors." We learned many life experiences in the ten short days of the trip that I will never forget. Our crew met our sailboat captain, Rick, and after introductions, he assigned us responsibilities for managing the boat and getting it ready to sail. We set sail at midnight, and hours later, I looked up to the sky and saw a billion stars that took my breath away. It made me think about how the universe could have created itself out of nothing, and I lost my thoughts when a huge wave hit us sideways, almost knocking me out of the captain's seat while four of us were on watch. Our group of twelve divided into four-person shifts, each covering the entire twelve hours it took us to cross the ocean.

Several times, our sailboat got thrown violently by waves, making me think about why I was out in the middle of the ocean at three o'clock in the morning steering the ship. We could be wiped out by a rogue wave at any time. Dr. Timothy stayed with us as long as he could, but after driving the university van for almost 18 hours straight from Cleveland, Ohio, to Miami, Florida, he retired to his bunk to get some much-needed sleep. It was a challenge for us amateurs on our first voyage, and I thought to myself, "Girl, you must be crazy to have let my roommate Samantha talk me into going on this wild trip."

After our three-hour watch was over, and another group of students took our place steering the ship, I dried myself off and went down the steps backward, as required on boats, hit my wooden slat, which was my bed, and fell asleep instantly from exhaustion. When I woke up, we had just docked in Bimini in the Bahamas, and it was so beautiful that I thought I was on another planet. The water was crystal clear, and I could see all the way to the bottom, with fish of all colors and shapes swimming in the water. The beach had crystal white sand, and native children were grabbing our lines and helping us tie them down on the dock. It was like a scene out of an H.G. Wells movie.

After our passports were approved by the customs officer, and the good doctor gave us permission to explore, Samantha and I scampered off like two kids in a candy store down the tiny island of Bimini. The island is only a few miles long and wide with a single road running the entire length of it. The friendly natives, standing outside their quaint shops, beckoned us to sample their wares and food. One of the pretty Bohemian women with a great big smile exclaimed, "Hey Mon, have I got a deal for you!" We indulged in ice cream, food, and straw hats. We saw fishermen bone fishing and children playing with dogs. We came across tiny bars, like the "End of the World Bar" situated at the far end of the strip where we tacked our t-shirts on the wall of the bar, as was the custom. We both tried the native drink called "Hurricane," and after three rounds, we were both down for the count, staggering back to the sailboat, where we passed out at 2 pm in the afternoon. Later that day, after waking up, we went swimming in the ocean and then visited the Hemmingway, a local bar named after the famous author Ernest Hemmingway, who had many sea and land adventures in the Bahamas and had written many of his novels on this island. Dr. John Timothy accompanied us to several pubs, as the legal drinking age in the Bahamas is 18. He nursed two beers and smoked a cigar while we partied. He confessed to being fairly religious and not believing in getting drunk or high, but he still stayed out with us, sharing stories and making sure we didn't do anything stupid. We drank a few shots of tequila, had some rum, and danced to Bob Marley's reggae music. At midnight, Dr. John Timothy gathered us as a group and made us head back to the ship. I later realized that he was looking out for us because he was not only our trip leader and responsible for us, but he also seemed to care about us. He set rules for us on the islands that we all agreed to, such as never going off alone with strangers, always exploring the islands in groups or teams, and ensuring that the women always had at least one guy with them. These rules might have seemed silly, but they made us feel safer, knowing that someone had our backs. The next day, we snorkeled on some beautiful reefs and saw hundreds of species of fish and corals. This was only our second day, with many more exciting experiences to come. We then sailed to the Berry Islands and on arrival, I thought this might be the most beautiful place on earth. Our group explored deserted islands where we built huge bonfires on the beaches and feasted on steaks and lobsters. We swam in the prettiest blue lagoons and had deserted beaches to ourselves. We climbed up cliffs and dove off them into blue holes. One day, a ship carrying students from the University of Michigan "Wolverines" came to the island where we had anchored off its coast. Even though we were "Buckeyes," we partied with them on an island we had all to ourselves. However, the thing that brought our group together the most and will be etched into my memory forever was on the final night before we were to sail back home.

Dr. John Timothy asked if we wanted to be initiated into the outdoor club. I was initially hesitant, remembering the obnoxious activities of my sorority's Hell Night. However, the good doctor explained that we had to come up with an outdoor club name for everyone in the group and tell a story about something they did on the trip that matched their behavior. It was all in good fun, and they named me "Hurricane Sarah" after the drinks Samantha and I had on the first day, which put us to sleep at 2 pm. The motion was moved and seconded, and I was now a member of the club with a new outdoor club name forever.

After everyone had been initiated, Dr. John Timothy shared his life story with us, explaining that he was fortunate to be alive, let alone leading outdoor trips with students. He had been given a death scare a few years earlier, but God had healed him. He went on to tell us that his outdoor club's name was El Presidente, Spanish for the President, given to him by another group of students on a similar trip. He loved the way we bonded as a group, helped each other through hardships, and broke down the wall of learning to trust between him as faculty/administrator and our group of students. He cared for us and felt a real tight bond between us all. He proceeded to tell us the details of his brush with death, which touched my heart for that moment in time.

He told us that several years before this trip, he had been diagnosed with a malignant tumor that was almost always fatal when found in men. He had to cancel the trip that year because he had undergone radical surgery, chemotherapy, and a multitude of tests to see if he would live or die. He had two young children ages 5 and 9 and prayed and asked God to spare his life so he could raise them as a Christian Father. He did not want his wife Francesca to lose her husband or have the enormous responsibility of raising their children as a single Mom. One night, while fearing for his life, waiting for lab reports that would tell him if he would live or die, Christ came to him on his bed and ministered to him. Christ overwhelmed him with a supernatural "peace" and "love" with the understanding that everything was going to be alright. Jesus spoke to him, stating "I have put you through some rough tests, but I am going to heal you." After this vision, he received only positive reports from his doctors, where before the vision, they warned him he would probably not survive. His oncologist doctor reviewed the latest report after his operation and said, "in Jewish terms you have received a miracle, and you are going to live!"

Dr. John Timothy warned us that someday we would have to make a decision to either follow Christ or reject him. I tucked this away for further analysis but soon forgot his message after returning to college and immersing myself in my coursework and the indoctrination of my liberal, atheist professors. I was not sure how they had such a hold on me, but I could not break their yoke around my belief system, for they had convinced me that evolution, not God, created everything.

Chapter 8

My Conservative Family

As I mentioned before, my parents, grandparents, brother, and sister all held a Christian conservative worldview, which differed from the liberal, atheist perspectives held by me and my professors. My parents, like Dr. John Timothy, believed that freedom was the most important thing for all people, and that the United States of America was the strongest, least racist nation in the world due to its strong Constitution, a population that still believed in God, and the tradition of strong family values. They pointed out that most people who lived in socialist states were repressed, controlled, or forbidden from practicing religion or believing in God, and they felt grateful for the freedoms offered in the United States. They were proud of their conservative views and vehemently opposed the idea of a one-world globalist government, which they believed would lead to disaster and the elimination of the freedoms enjoyed in this country.

My brother Josh and grandpa Pops loved spending time outdoors, hunting, fishing, hiking, whitewater rafting, rock climbing, and camping. Their shared interests helped them to become close, and I sometimes felt jealous of their bond. In an effort to grow closer to them, I joined them on outdoor trips whenever possible. One particularly memorable trip was when Pops, Josh, and I went on an outdoor excursion to the New River Gorge in West Virginia. We contracted with Rivermen Outfitters, who provided us with unique and fun outdoor experiences from Wednesday through Sunday. They trained and took us on mountain hikes and biking trails on Wednesday and Thursday. On Friday, they taught us to rock climb on cliffs overlooking the beautiful New River Gorge. On Saturday, we practiced paddling skills, worked as a team, and learned our river guide's commands on the New River. On Sunday, after proving our proficiency in rafting skills, Josh, Pops, and I were allowed to raft the technical and dangerous Gulley River. It was an incredible experience, and I felt grateful for the opportunity to learn new skills, work as a team, and have fun with my brother and grandfather.

After my Bahamas trip and this West Virginia excursion, I developed a greater appreciation for the need to preserve our environment. Professor John Timothy, Pops, and Josh all emphasized the importance of having clean oceans, lakes, and rivers that are free of pesticides, pollutants, and contaminants. Despite their conservative beliefs, they felt strongly that industry and government must work together to clean up air and water pollution. They called for the creation of wetlands and game preserves to help waterfowl and other animals survive and flourish. They encouraged reforestation and better forest management for the ecological survival of the planet. The outdoors held a special place in their hearts, and they wanted their children and grandchildren to enjoy it for years to come. They advocated for a balance between preserving our national parks and the need to keep our nation energy-efficient and maintain jobs.

In contrast, my father and mother believed that keeping people employed and the nation energy-sufficient at all costs should be the nation's focus. They believed that the United States of America should continue to be the world leader in energy production and that, as cheaper fossil fuels were slowly being used up, we could expedite the development of solar, wind, and other reusable energy sources to take their place. Although my parents, brother, and grandfather disagreed on how to balance environmental issues with the need to keep people working, they were able to work out their differences through open dialogue and listening to each other's viewpoints. It was unfortunate that the rest of the nation couldn't seem to come to an agreement on anything.

During my college years, my liberal professors preached about the need to stop destroying forests, abandon oil pipelines, and use only reusable, clean, and environmentally friendly resources. They were of the ideology that the government must force us to go green, regardless of the cost, and believed that all fossil fuels should be outlawed, with only reusable resources such as wind power being used. They advocated for electric cars and did not care if people lost their jobs due to these policies, believing that it was the government's responsibility, not the private sector's, to provide jobs and support the population.

My parents, Dr. Timothy, and Josh held the belief that the government existed to provide services and security for its citizens and was not responsible for creating jobs. As I mentioned earlier, neither side was entirely correct and the refusal of conservatives and liberals to collaborate with each other prevented any meaningful progress towards preventing environmental catastrophes. This confusion allowed deep state globalists to slowly push their agenda on everyone.

Both right-wing extremists and left-wing extremists were equally guilty of ignoring environmental preservation, with the former focused solely on industry and job creation. In response to the left's offer to save the planet, I jumped on the bandwagon and supported the Paris Agreement, which limited air pollution that the United States and other countries were pumping into the atmosphere. However, I was not aware until later that many countries that signed the accord never intended to comply with its demands. China and Russia were among the worst offenders, continuing to pump hydrocarbons into the air despite their commitment to the accords. They knew that the United States, by giving up its energy independence, would eventually become weakened, as it would have to purchase green technology from foreign countries at much higher prices.

At that time, like most people on the planet, I was naive about what was happening behind the scenes.

Chapter 9

How the New World Order Leader was Created

Alexander was born in Moldovia, a small country in Europe. His parents, Jarrad and Madoc, were wealthy and had significant political and corporate power in Moldovia. Before Alexander was born, they searched for brilliant scientists with knowledge of genetic engineering to develop a son with superior genetics, physical strength, and intellectual abilities. Hexitron, a powerful corporation led by Jarrad, provided the scientists who created Alexander through genetic splicing of DNA taken from the world's most gifted people. The embryo was then implanted into a surrogate mother who carried the baby until birth. After his birth, he was named Alexander Dimitrov.

Madoc, who had an important position in the government of Moldovia, taught Alexander their socialist, corporate, and occultist doctrine from the time he was six years old until he was a mature adult. Madoc's and Jarrad's philosophy was that people are like sheep who need to be led by shepherds with superior intellect, knowledge, and power. Some of the knowledge Alexander's parents taught him came from occult spiritualism. They searched globally for the most powerful witches and spiritualists to teach and train Alexander in the dark arts. They also prayed for power and wisdom from the Dark Lord, who appeared to them in dreams and promised to make them powerful world leaders if they would give their lives and souls to him. The Dark Lord asked for one more thing in return, which was to dedicate their only son Alexander to him. In return, the Dark Lord would make them powerful world leaders and their son Alexander the leader of the future Dark Lord's World Empire. They accepted this proposal enthusiastically.

Madoc taught Alexander all the secrets of government manipulations, including how to use political power to crush opponents, become rich through graft, deal making, and bribery, spread lies against enemies, manipulate world currency, and use news networks, social media, and communication as tools for corporate and government propaganda and takeover. Jarrad taught Alexander the Hexitron corporation secrets, including how to manipulate world stock exchanges and bond markets to maximize profits, gain advantage over business competition through stealing secrets through corporate espionage, use illegal insider trader information to manipulate stocks for investors to achieve maximum profits, corner the market on valuable minerals needed for the new "green movement," exploit the governments of the world for inflated prices because of its insatiable desire to build clean energy power plants, power grids, windmills, and electrical batteries, and especially use lobbyists to make huge donations to campaigns of government officials in return for government contracts and favors.

Alexander's lifetime leadership training, his superior intellect, his knowledge of government and corporations, and his knowledge of occult spiritualism helped him learn how to become a global entrepreneur. He used his knowledge and cunning to develop a plan to purchase the world's cheaper fossil fuels for energy use while the rest of the world wanted expensive wind, battery, and solar power. By using Hexitron and the Moldovia government to purchase the world's cheaper energy resources of oil, gas, coal, and uranium, he controlled much of the world's energy reserves. He also cornered the market on metallic elements such as cobalt, manganese, and nickel necessary for the high demand to make environmentally friendly batteries, enabling him to make these prices extremely expensive in the future. This inconspicuous leader from a small country in Europe had plans to become the leader of all nations.

Alexander kept his knowledge about power and energy from dark sources a secret from the world. His true allegiance was to his master, the Dark Lord, who had empowered him. Alexander Dimitrov, the unknown leader, was intelligent and charismatic, and soon he would claim to have all the answers to the world's problems after the Dark Lord's predicted collapse of the world markets. His plan included methodically purchasing much of the global communications, media networks, and power grids using his parents and his own power and influence over the Hexitron Corporation and their connections with the Moldovian government. In return, he would share his message of peace and prosperity with the global community and control much of its energy resources. In truth, he was a power-hungry, sadistic megalomaniac whose only desire was to control the world. He received power from the dark forces through the occult, surrounding himself with witches and spiritualists. The Dark Lord provided Alexander with a powerful spiritualist named Abaddon, and together they had a mutual goal to unite all the world's religions. At Abaddon's urging, Alexander gave a power seat to all the world religions, including Islam, Buddhism, Hinduism, Sikhism,

Shinto, Taoism, Confucianism, and Zoroastrianism, on the New World Order Council of Religion. This was their way of creating a powerful one-world religion that pretended to unite all the world's religions, with the exclusion of Judaism and Christianity, which they had condemned as heretical. Judaism would not be invited, as Israel was hated by the Supreme Leader, and Christianity had lost all relevance after the disappearance of millions of its believers throughout the world on one day. Therefore, there would be very few people who believed in Christianity to fight for inclusion into the New World Order Council of Religion. Another part of Alexander's plan was to declare Christians non-entities who must be blamed for causing the world's collapse and chaos; therefore, Christianity and the Bible would be outlawed.

For many years, the globalists had convinced the global community that all religions were basically the same, with nobody's god or gods being superior. Therefore, it was easy for Alexander and Abaddon to convince the world's religious leaders that love, peace, and unity with the people of a global society should replace strict religious doctrines.

Chapter 10

Sarah- I lost My Way

Now, once again, back to my story of how a liberal atheist ended up here in prison, awaiting trial for believing in Christianity. My grandfather, Pops, and grandmother, "Granny," taught Sunday school and Bible classes for years in their church and on their YouTube channel. Pops did most of the preaching and teaching, while Granny helped him by diligently preparing awesome Christian worship songs before Pops taught his lessons. She gave him advice on how to present his material with love and compassion while still conveying the spiritual and biblical meaning. They proved to be an awesome team and convinced my mother, father, brother, and sister that, in order to go to heaven someday, one had to repent of their sins to God, believe in their heart that Jesus Christ was God's only Son, died for their sins, and was resurrected from the dead. The whole family made Jesus Lord and Savior of their lives.

Well, I had slowly lost my faith over the years, or maybe I never really believed in God, as my faith now was based on the science of evolution. After all, these brilliant progressive professors had convinced me that all things came about through evolutionary processes and adaptation that happened over millions of years. The Bible claimed that all things were created by God in seven days, which was hard for me to comprehend. The only person that had an explanation of this process of creation that made sense to me was my friend, Professor Dr. John Timothy. He said to me, "Sarah, the scriptures say that a day to the Lord is like a thousand days to people, as He lives in heaven where there is no such thing as time." He also said to me, "God is so powerful and has such infinite knowledge that it was very possible he created the heavens, earth, animals, plant life, and people in seven days. He probably planned this creation for thousands of years and then decided to make it happen."

Pops and Granny agreed with the Doc's theory of creation, and they also cautioned me that the Bible warned of a time when God would send Jesus back to punish the wicked. "Sarah," they said, "we are living in what God calls the 'end of time,' and I believe that Jesus is coming back soon, perhaps even in our lifetime, to gather all the people who believe in Him up into the air and take them to heaven. The Bible calls this the Rapture. Please accept Jesus as your Savior and Lord, so that if Jesus comes back during our lifetime, you will go to heaven in the Rapture with us. After all the believers in Christ disappear, the Antichrist will take over the world. He will call for peace, and act as if he has all the answers to the world's problems. He will seem like a great, loving person with charismatic qualities and be a skilled orator, but inwardly he is a ravenous wolf who wants to murder and kill anyone who disagrees with him. His real goal is to rule the world. According to the Bible, he will accomplish this over a period of seven years. He will make a peace treaty with Israel for the first three and a half years. After gaining complete control of food, supplies, markets, and armies, he will have absolute power. He will then break the treaty with Israel, enter the newly built Jewish Temple, and slay a pig on the altar of God (which is an abomination to God). He will then reveal his true nature, declaring himself as God, and rule for three and a half more years, during which his reign will be hell on earth for anyone who is left behind after the Rapture. He will force everyone to receive a "Mark" on their right hand or forehead, declaring allegiance to him as God and bowing down to him. This Mark is 666 and stands for the Beast. Failure to receive this mark of absolute and utter subservience to him will mean that one can no longer buy or sell food, products, clothes, or anything else. But I must warn you, Sarah, if you take this Mark, you can never be saved, and God's wrath will soon follow. After allowing this madman, full of Satanic power, to reign for seven years, Jesus Christ will come back and destroy the Antichrist, his armies, and all those who served him. Then the wrath of God, as predicted through John the Apostle in Revelation (the last book of the Bible), will come down on the earth, and it will be a horrific judgment on people who have rejected Him so corruptly and for so long. Sarah, I implore you to accept Jesus now as your Lord and Savior, so that you won't be left behind. If you are left behind after the Rapture takes place, please do not receive the Mark of the Beast. Again, it will be the number 666, which represents the Antichrist or the Beast of Revelation."

Oh, how I wish I had believed my Grandpa, Grandma, Dad, Mom, Sister, and Brother. Oh, how I wish I had believed Dr. John Timothy and chosen to believe in Christ over those other arrogant and pompous God-hating professors. How could I have been so stupid? When the Christians all disappeared on that fateful day, I knew immediately that I had made the wrong choice, rejecting God and believing all the lies of the globalists, world-order proponents, atheists, and evolutionary scientists.

Chapter 11

Sarah is Transformed

I was done with the lies. I got down on my knees and cried out to God, "Please forgive me, for I am a terrible sinner! You are the Creator of the worlds, the God of my father, mother, sister, brother, grandmothers, and grandfathers. Jesus, you are God's Holy Son who died for me. Please forgive me of my sins and come into my heart." God heard me and immediately gave me a supernatural love and peace for other people. I was a new creation in Him and was prepared to die for Him, as I was not going to bow down to the Supreme Leader, his Prophet, or receive the Mark of the Beast.

But now, I had a dilemma. How was I going to survive without being able to buy or sell food? How could I withstand the strength of this evil empire? Who could protect me from the wicked court system and the young, zealous people who were turning in everyone who believed in God? These young teenagers who had gone to the New World Order education camps were so indoctrinated that they were turning in their parents, siblings, and even their best friends when they refused to comply with accepting a one-world government and the new religion of the Prophet Abaddon. Abaddon was declaring that the Supreme Leader was the true Messiah and actually God himself.

To make the Supreme Leader appear as God, Abaddon disbanded the New World Council of Religion and had its leaders thrown in jail for blasphemy. From now on, only Alexander was to be worshiped. This caused the Islamic followers to rebel, as they had been secretly planning a coup d'état of the Supreme Leader to install their chosen Messiah or Prophet as the new world leader.

Chapter 12

The Rise of Magog

After millions disappeared, the country of Russia ceased to exist as its government collapsed along with its money, power grids, and communication systems. Out of the chaos arose a new military Chiefdom and Islamic Cleric named Magog, who united the former countries of ancient Islam including Russia, Turkey, Iran, Sudan, Iraq, and Libya. Magog called for a Jihad against the world, seeking to bring all people under his Islamic Government. He demanded that all former Islamic countries unite and defeat the infidels, and day by day his army grew larger.

Magog's followers gathered secretly at first, and then openly with a fierce determination to come against Israel. They planned to destroy the infidel Supreme Leader, his Prophet, and the New World Order if the peace treaty between Israel and the New World Order continued. They never believed in the New World Religion Council or its Prophet Abaddon. Magog considered himself a Prince of the former kingdoms of Persia and Babylon and soon named Ishmael as his consultant and Holy

Prophet.

Together they considered the Supreme Leader of the New World Order and his false prophet Abaddon as false prophets who had made blasphemous statements against their God Allah and the one True Prophet Mohamed. They used this blasphemy as justification to rally their armies and come against Israel, which had made a treaty with the Supreme Leader. They had always hated Israel, and now their goal was to cut off the head of the two infidel snakes, namely Israel and the New World Order.

The Islamists gathered a multi-million-man army and came storming down from the North as a vast horde to the Israeli border, where they were met by the government of Israel and the New World Order armies. The peace treaty that the New World Order had made with Israel would bring both their destruction.

Chapter 13

The First Great Battle

The Supreme Leader now faced a Muslim Jihadist army closing in on Jerusalem due to the entangling peace treaty he had made with Israel. Seeking aid, Alexander turned to his spiritual leader Abaddon, who consulted with the most powerful and trusted witches and spiritualists to ask for help from the Dark Lord. The Dark Lord responded by enlisting his most powerful demonic powers and principalities from spiritual high places to protect Alexander's military with unseen demonic forces. Abaddon predicted a great victory over Magog, his followers, and army.

Despite his plan to eventually break the treaty due to his hatred towards the Jews, Alexander kept the peace treaty with Israel because he could not tolerate Magog's threat to his world empire. He assembled his world armies to fight and destroy this threat to his kingdom and throne.

In the battle, the Israelites were placed on the front lines against the hordes from the North, where they suffered massive casualties. Alexander kept his army at the rear of the battle lines to ensure that the Jews took the brunt of the fighting, decreasing their fighting force as much as possible. The battle raged on, devastating both sides, with hundreds of thousands lying dead on the fields outside of Jerusalem.

Then, a mighty earthquake struck underneath the main portion of Magog's army, causing the ground to open up and swallow hundreds of thousands of his men. Over half of Magog's army fell into the earth and died in the destruction that followed. Magog attempted to rally his troops, but he couldn't communicate with his generals. Hailstones and fire rained down from heaven, causing interference and distortion of his Military Encrypted Secure Smartphones.

Magog's troops who had escaped the earthquake and killing thousands started to murder each other, thinking that they were the enemy. It was as if Allah himself had deserted them and some unknown God was now causing havoc and utter destruction of his once great army. In this mass hysteria, Magog's troops were soon reduced to less than 1000, who then surrendered to Israel's and the Supreme Leader's troops.

Upon hearing of the surrender, Alexander argued with the Israeli generals, who demanded mercy for all the prisoners. However, Alexander ordered that they all be slaughtered without mercy. The devastation was severe, and the news and social media showed pictures of wild beasts and birds feasting on the carcasses of rotting corpses.

The Supreme Leader positioned the head of Magog atop a pole, raised over the highest point of the Jewish Temple. He then accused Israel of being responsible for the war and devastation, claiming that they hated the Islamists. With the Israeli armies weakened by the fierce battle and using the false pretext that Israel had disobeyed his orders and executed the remaining prisoners of Magog, Alexander ordered his troops to surround the Israeli army and force their surrender. The Israeli forces, greatly outnumbered and unable to use their nuclear arsenal with the New World Army situated directly above them, had no choice but to capitulate. However, a significant number of Israelites refused to surrender and fought their way to a secret passageway that led to the mountains and away from the NOW army.

As the Israeli Prime Minister Aaron Deyan was unable to escape and surrendered, he was brought before Alexander to answer for false accusations. Aaron noticed Alexander's angry countenance, which appeared demonic. Although Alexander had planned it all along, now that he was in control of the world's greatest army and could not be stopped, he ordered Aaron to "get down on your knees and explain to me, was it your God, the old God of Abraham, Isaac, and Jacob, who caused this great earthquake? If it was the God of Israel, then thank him for me as I now control the majority of the world's armies, including what's left of yours. Some of your traitors escaped to the mountains, but I will soon destroy them also." Aaron refused to bow down before Alexander's throne and said, "Yes, the earthquake was caused by the God of Israel, and I refuse to bow down to anyone but my God, who is the creator of heaven and earth and will soon punish you for your blasphemy!"

As the whole world watched on the NWO Cable News Network, Alexander's countenance changed from peaceful to full-blown hatred and rage, and he ripped up the Treaty with Israel. The Supreme Leader then ordered his executioner to kill Aaron. The executioner, who loved his work due to his demented nature, used an ancient Assyrian sword to behead Aaron in front of the cameras for the whole world to see. Alexander then ordered Aaron's head to be placed beside Magog's at the top of the temple.

Chapter 14

The Supreme Leader Evolves

After defeating his hated enemy Magog and breaking the peace alliance with Israel, Supreme Leader Alexander Dimitrov was empowered by his mighty victory and moved closer to his goal of creating a world empire. Though the Israeli army had fled to the mountains, he planned to eliminate them completely.

To insult the Jewish religion and its followers, Alexander Dimitrov boldly entered the Holy Jewish Temple, which had been allowed to be rebuilt as part of the original peace treaty with Israel. He proceeded to sacrifice a pig on the Jewish altar, an act considered the most horrific a gentile could commit.

As he exited the Temple with blood dripping from his hands, Alexander addressed the world on NWO Cable News, declaring himself to be "Alexander The Beast, the God of this World." The Prophet Abaddon bowed down and worshiped him, urging all the people of the world to do the same.

A statue of the Supreme Leader, called Alexander the Beast, was erected outside Jerusalem with the number 666 placed on its forehead, symbolizing Alexander's evolution from man to God. The Israeli army remained a minor threat, but Alexander's power over the world was now absolute.

Some brave Israelites then followed through with their plot to assassinate the Supreme Leader. Jeremiah Sharon, an Israeli patriot and master marksman, was selected by these Israeli patriots to kill the blasphemer, Alexander. Jeremiah found a secure place to set up his long rifle on top of a mountain over 1500 meters away from where the Supreme Leader was to present himself to the world as the conqueror of the fearless jihadist Magog of the North. Jeremiah raised his Galil Sniper Rifle and looked through his Zeiss Conquest V4 Scope, with his spotter calculating the exact distance to the target and making adjustments for wind speed. He aimed, said a prayer, and slowly pulled the trigger. The shot hit the Supreme Leader's head. The crowd hushed and was stunned as he slumped down in his chariot that he had built just for this celebration.

Jeremiah and the Israeli assassination team were quickly discovered, brutally tortured, and then hung from the entrance gate to Jerusalem. Alexander was quietly moved to his capital city, Babylon, where he was not expected to live from his wound. In retaliation for this shooting, Abaddon then declared that all Israeli military personnel who had surrendered be executed. Thousands of Jews were then slaughtered. The only Israeli military personnel to escape the New World Order militia were those who fled to the mountains of Jordan and hid in caves.

The NWO News declared Alexander's death a great tragedy and called for a week of mourning. As the world grieved for its Supreme Leader, a supposed miracle occurred. Three days after his death, he suddenly and miraculously recovered from his head wound, rose up, and addressed the world once again, proclaiming himself as the Messiah and God. The Prophet once again declared that everyone in the world who had not yet received the Mark must show their allegiance to the Supreme Leader by receiving his Mark of 666 on their right hand or forehead. This would be the final declaration from everyone receiving the Mark that they believed Alexander was their Messiah, King, and God.

Alexander and the Prophet had secretly placed a monitoring and tracking device in computerized chips inside the Mark, which enabled his leadership team's supercomputer to track and monitor their movements. Anyone who wished to buy or sell food or products must now have the Mark, or they would face starvation. This efficient and orderly system enabled the world to operate under one cashless system. However, failure to receive "The Mark" would be equivalent to insurrection, and people would be held accountable for this provocation.

Most people believed that since Alexander had come back from the dead, he must be a God, and receiving the Mark was an honor. They found the system efficient and harmless. My suspicion was that his death and resurrection were staged to ensure that those who originally did not believe in him would convert. Perhaps he used a body double on the day he was supposed to have been killed. Even if the real God had allowed this man's resurrection, claiming now to be God (who was full of hate, fury, and the devil), he would never be a god to me. Together with the Prophet, they were performing magic. They say you will "know a person or leader by their fruits," but after the massacre of millions of people who refused to receive the "Mark" and follow this evil man or his evil Prophet, his fruit proved to be pure evil!

Chapter 15

Sarah-Turns Evangelist

Getting back to my dilemma, I knew I was not going to bow down to the World Ruler or worship him as God, nor receive 'The Mark,' which I now realized was the Mark of the Beast as prophesied by John the Apostle in the Bible. This was the proof that God was real, as the Bible had predicted all this evil that was happening exactly as my parents and grandparents had warned me. I now believed that the disappearance of millions of people that caused some of this chaos was actually Christians being raptured to be with Jesus before the Antichrist would appear. I was not going to make the same mistake I originally made by believing atheists and foolish people who thought this crazy leader was God.

As I mentioned earlier, I got down on my knees and prayed to ask God to forgive my sins, including rejecting Him for many years, and to ask God to come into my heart. I reconfirmed my commitment to serve God for the rest of my life. I was the Lord's servant now and forever, a born-again, Holy Spirit-filled Christian. I might have to starve to death, but I would only bow to

God the Father, Son, and Holy Ghost, who make up the Trinity and are my God forever. I expect to die for my faith and be reunited with my family in heaven soon, but for now, I want to live long enough to warn anyone who will listen that the Prophet Abaddon and Alexander the Supreme Leader are false prophets controlled by the devil. This is my mission, and I am willing to die for my God. I will no longer be ashamed of the Gospel of Christ. With God's help, I can get people saved before God takes me home. Little did I know, but my story was just beginning.

By refusing 'The Mark' and refusing to bow down to this Satan-filled leader and his Prophet, I had a death warrant on my head, and I had to find a way to eat and live. As a reminder, my family was all gone as the Lord had taken them in the Rapture. One of my best friends, Rebecca, had gone to the dark side and knew I was refusing 'The Mark.' She proceeded to turn me into the authorities, and there was now a reward and price on my head for insurrection. I was wanted dead or alive. She had received the 'Mark' and felt it was her duty to turn me in (and it was profitable to do so) after I had confessed to her that I was now a follower of Jesus Christ. All religions, and especially Christianity, were now banned throughout the world as decreed by the Prophet Abaddon, who the few people that were rebelling, like myself, called the 'Little Beast.' I escaped to the mountains surrounding Jerusalem, where I met more people who chose to be part of the rebellion.

The rebellion was made up of anyone who did not believe in the New World Order government and did not receive its Mark. Many people, including former Israeli military personnel who had escaped the Battle of Magog, 144,000 Jews who now believed Jesus Christ was their Messiah, and just ordinary people like me who hated the NWO, were part of the rebellion. God sent Two

Witnesses from heaven to earth to witness against the Prophet and the Supreme Leader. They were also charged to preach salvation to anyone who had not yet received the 'Mark of the Beast.' They said that the Supreme Leader was 'The Antichrist,' a man filled with Satan himself, and that the Prophet was a man who was possessed by powerful demons.

Chapter 16

The Two Witnesses

The Two Witnesses, who wore sackcloths, had actually come from heaven and were given power by God to perform miracles and signs that would convert the unsaved. God told them that they must prophesy against The Antichrist and his prophet for 1260 days, be killed by the beast, and their bodies should be left to rot in the streets. After three and a half days, they would rise from the dead in full view of the world and return to heaven. They secretly revealed to us that they had never died when they were on earth originally, but were taken to heaven centuries before to be trained by Jesus Christ in what they were to do and say to confront the wicked Prophet and the Antichrist. They were also giving the people of the earth a final warning to accept Jesus Christ as their Lord and Savior or face terrible judgment. One Witness was named Elijah, and the other was named Enoch. The Two Witnesses exclaimed, "We will eventually be martyred for our faith in Christ, as will all 144,000 Jewish Christians who will also be God's witnesses." They warned the rest of us who had joined this rebellion, stating, 'Have no doubt that following Jesus and us may lead to your deaths, as we are facing more than just men, but as the

Apostle Paul warned, "we fight against powers and principalities of darkness in high places." Some people then left the group and went away sadly, unwilling to die for the cause. However, the majority of us declared in a loud voice, "We will follow you, and if the Lord asks us to die beside you for Christ's sake, we will do so willingly!"

We then broke off into teams and spread throughout Israel, declaring the Good News of the Gospel throughout the land. To our amazement, many of the Jewish people we witnessed to were declaring Christ as their Messiah and Savior. They refused to get 'The Mark,' and many were thrown into jail. The Two Witnesses, after witnessing throughout most of Israel, went to the steps of the modern-day rebuilt Jewish Temple and started preaching and performing miracles. The New World Order Cable News was broadcasting this event to the whole world, as a huge debate was taking place between the Two Witnesses and the Prophet Abaddon. The Two Witnesses were shouting to the people with great power and authority that there was only one God, who existed as the Father, Son, and Holy Ghost. They brought fire down from heaven as a sign of their authority. They proclaimed Jesus as the Savior of the world, who died for everyone's sins. They preached repentance and baptism in the name of Jesus, and the need to receive everlasting light. They quoted the Bible verse John 3:16, "For God so loved the world that he gave his only begotten Son, that whosoever believeth in him should not perish but have everlasting life." People who were sick, and some who were dying, were brought before Elijah and Enoch, and they proclaimed, 'In the name of Jesus, be healed!' And they were healed.

Chapter 17

The Prophet Abaddon

The Prophet Abaddon, also known as the Little Beast, had been commanded by the Supreme Leader to travel to Jerusalem and disrupt the healings and miracles performed by the Two Witnesses. Meanwhile, the Supreme Leader himself was attending to important New World Order business in his new capital, New Babylon. Abaddon had brought with him a powerful group of witches, spiritualists, and Satanists to discredit the Two Witnesses and their work for Christ.

The Supreme Leader once again blamed the Two Witnesses for the collapse of the world system, accusing them of causing the disappearance of many people that led to the world banks' collapse. He then ordered the sorcerers and witches to cast spells and create delusions to disrupt the crowd, who were in attendance. However, these spells and incantations had no effect on people who had not received the Mark. Those who had received the Mark started prophesying, shouting down, and screaming at the Two Witnesses, declaring they would destroy them.

The Two Witnesses spoke the word "peace," and a hush fell over the crowd. All those in pain were quickly healed, and they were now free from pain. The witches and sorcerers countered by having some people levitate into the air. Some used hypnotism to make their own followers do crazy things. Some sorcerers spewed fire from their mouths, and some fanatics cut themselves and went into hypnotic trances and started prophesying demonic decrees.

The New World Order Cable News Network, however, broadcasted only the pandemonium that occurred from the occultists and not the healings and miracles brought on by the Two Witnesses. The fake NWO news twisted all the good that was happening from God's Holy witnesses and focused only on the bravado of the false prophets and praised the leadership of these crazed fanatics. The Witnesses were said to have caused insurrection and should be punished for crimes against the world.

The Supreme Leader, also known as the Beast, watched the confusion on his NWO Cable News on his throne in New Babylon and smiled. Some of his followers heard him laugh like that of a jackal that had just feasted on its prey. He would soon deliver his final solution plan to the world for the distribution of food and other commodities to ensure that all who worshiped him and received the Mark would receive their goods and services. Of course, he knew that all who had received the Mark had also received a microchip that would give his regime valuable information on where they were spending their time, money, and with whom.

Due to the overpopulation of the planet and the resulting scarcity of food, the Dark Lord planned to kill all those over the age of 60 and those with physical and mental disabilities as a sacrifice to ensure there was enough food to provide for his most ardent supporters. The Dark Lord had laid out his plans while Alexander was in a self-induced coma after narrowly avoiding a head wound. The plan worked out perfectly when an Israeli shot him, the bullet piercing the top of his skull but missing any vital brain matter. His doctors immediately placed him into an induced coma to prevent any swelling on the brain.

While Alexander was comatose, he secretly confessed to his most loyal followers, 'I instructed the Prophet and my doctors to inform the world that I was brain dead with no hope of recovery.' Several days later, when he emerged from the coma, he discovered that the world was already mourning his death. Alexander continued, 'When I appeared on my NWO Cable News Network, pronounced alive and well by my doctors, I informed everyone that I had been brought back from the dead. The mourning turned to celebration in the streets. What a bunch of fools they were!'

Now that Alexander had received his instructions from the Dark Lord, he was preparing to destroy the remnants of Israel once and for all, showing no mercy to the Israelites and taking no prisoners. With the exception of the two foolish witnesses, their 144,000 Jewish Christian followers, and the Jewish military personnel who had escaped into the mountains, the world was his.

Alexander continued, "I will also destroy the Chinese military who had been resurrected after Zang Wei established his rule over China. The Dark Lord gave me a plan to throw anyone who had refused the Mark into re-education camps or prosecute them as insurrectionists. In these camps, they would be given a second chance to extinguish their religious beliefs or be killed. Through The Prophet Abaddon, I will declare that there is only one God - Alexander the Beast - and one religious leader - Abaddon, The Prophet. I killed my doctors with my own bare hands by strangulation so that there were no witnesses of my death and fake resurrection. The Prophet cremated their bodies. With the knowledge and power granted to me by the Dark Lord, we will rule the world together. While I was in a coma, the Dark Lord took me to his throne room and not only filled me with his power but also shared his plans to rule the world. Once the re-education camps were established and in full operation, I was to set up a tribunal system of courts with hand-selected judges who would decide the fate of all those who refused to get the Mark or bow down to me as their god and ruler. Those who did not repent of their apostasy would be killed and beheaded as a warning that refusing my rule would have severe consequences. My father, the Dark Lord, gave me these commands and promised to enter me so that we could rule the world forever. The tribunals were devised specifically to rid us of the remainder of the 144,000 and those who believed in the Jewish God and their messiah, Jesus Christ.

According to the Dark Lord's plan, we first outlawed the Christian religion and belief in the Father, Son, and Holy Ghost, and we also made it illegal to own or read the Bible. We paid people good money to track down and burn Bibles, and we offered rewards of $500 per person for anyone who turned in someone that was a believer in Christ, refused to get the Mark due to their religious beliefs, or would not worship me. The Dark Lord taught me to cause hatred between all the races by blaming all the opposing opponents as racists and haters. We also made policies that encouraged all the children in the New World Order indoctrination program to declare that all sexual genders are now accepted. They could now decide to be a boy if they were a girl and change to a girl if they were created a boy. They could also declare themselves transgender or even an animal if they chose to. However, the main reason for this policy was to cause confusion among the children and go against Christian belief that boys or girls were created by God to be male or female and should accept and embrace their gender.

The Dark Lord instructed me to force New World Order scientists to continue developing new viruses, along with vaccines to counter the viruses and protect New World Order members. These viruses would rid the world of anyone who did not get the Mark, as they were traitors, and aid in population control. As the New World Order was to be a one-world government, a decree was to be announced over the Global News Network that no longer would there be any national borders. Any former country's nationalism would now be illegal, and all borders were declared open.

The Dark Lord gave me the most important order of all, which was to ask him to take over my body, soul, and mind by asking him to come into me. This was the only way to defeat the Two Witnesses and annihilate their followers. I obeyed gladly, and together his power and my wicked humanity could not be matched. Together we could defeat the God of heaven. Satan, the Dark Lord, proceeded to enter me after I asked him to come in, and now together, we had unbelievable power and authority.

"According to the Dark Lord, the Two Witnesses had placed a protective covering over all Christian believers left after the Rapture, including the 144,000. The Dark Lord finally acknowledged the Rapture of the Christian believers that occurred years before. However, this growing insurgency of the Christian faith posed a major threat to the New World Order. The Witnesses used their power to call down fire from the heavens to destroy anyone who endangered them. With Satan empowering me, we were going to destroy the Two Witnesses. Only then could we proceed with our plans to arrest their followers, try them for treason, and kill them all.

The Dark Lord also gave me a plan to eliminate the final two threats to our world kingdom: China and the remnants of the Israeli army who had escaped into the hills. We would make a peace pact with China in which the New World Order would reconstruct their cyber network and communication systems, and in return, China would use its military to destroy the remnants of the Israeli army, thereby ridding the world of Jews forever. Then Alexander would turn the NWO armies against China after they had been weakened by fighting the Israelites in the mountains."

Chapter 18

Sarah the Zealot

Here I was, Sarah, a born-again zealot of Jesus Christ,
preaching the Gospel day and night on street corners, alleyways,
the Temple Steps, and all over Israel. Protected by the Two
Witnesses, together with other Christians, we were a strong and
mighty army of God. I screamed, "Repent, be baptized in the name
of the Father, Son, and Holy Ghost, and be saved." To my
amazement, many people, mostly Jewish, who had not received the
Mark, were converting to Christianity. The Two Witnesses were
powerfully bringing down fire from heaven, healing people, and
declaring that this was the last chance to accept Christ as Lord and
Savior before the wrath of God would come upon all men and
women who did not repent of their wicked deeds. Those who had
already received 'The Mark' hatefully screamed at us, calling us
blasphemers, racists, and haters. It was a great time to be filled with
the Spirit of the 'Living God' as we used God's power to bind and
cast out evil spirits by the thousands. This effort was carried on by
the 144,000 alongside those disciples recently converted to Christ,
not only in Israel but throughout the globe. It was a war, and we
were not afraid of the Dark Lord, Supreme Leader, The Prophet,

or any of their followers because God was giving us the words to speak with His power and authority.

Just when we were at our greatest strength, it all suddenly and tragically ended when the Two Witnesses, whose special time of witnessing to the world had come to a close by God, were slain on the steps of the Temple. Witnesses swore that it was Satan incarnate himself, living in the Supreme Leader (The Beast), and the Prophet (Little Beast), who was filled with over a thousand demons. They combined their strength, took two giant ancient Assyrian swords, and slew the Two Witnesses. For the first time, as the whole world witnessed their deaths on the New World Cable News, I, Sarah, the Zealot for Christ's kingdom, was forced to run and hide with other Christians back into our camps in the mountains where we would regroup and plan our next moves. We had to do this as mobs of angry followers of Alexander and Abaddon were murdering anyone who did not have the Mark. They chanted, "Death to all those who oppose the Supreme Leader and his prophet!" Soon there were thousands of martyrs killed in the streets! The witches and Satanists cried out as they slaughtered innocent people, "Let their blood be on us." Most of the original 144,000 Jewish Christians who were not initially killed by the crowds were rounded up and thrown into jails, prisons, and internment camps throughout the world as they would not back down and stop preaching Jesus Christ as Lord and Savior. Many were brought before tribunals without due process and immediately sentenced to death by corrupt judges. I was willing to die with them, but several of my new converts convinced me to live to witness another day.

We disguised our faces and blended in with many refugees fleeing to the mountains where we hid in caves and had to hunt wild animals to survive. At our base camp hidden in the mountains, I experienced the love of other believers in Christ. Now I understood how my family had loved each other in Christ along with their church brothers and sisters before they were raptured. Here we were outcasts with little food and only the probability that we would be martyred for our faith, but we were in unity and harmony. We shared our food, faith, and hope that Jesus was going to come back and destroy the Antichrist (Supreme Leader) and his million-person war machine

We were a diverse group of individuals, consisting of both males and females, once wealthy and impoverished, from every nationality, race, and ethnicity, all unified in our faith in Christ.

Chapter 19

Almeria- Alexander's Original Rise to Power

Almeria hailed from the same small country as Alexander Dimitrov - Moldovia, the same Alexander who now proclaimed himself as God. Almeria shared a detailed account of Alexander's ascent to power, how he deceived and conquered not only Moldovia but also the entire world. Alexander was an unknown figure when he emerged in Moldovia as the Minister of Natural Resources, taking over the position from his late father, Madoc. He struck a deal with a foreign investment group called Hexitron, which discovered the world's richest deposit of nickel, cobalt, and other minerals in the land that Moldovia controlled. These minerals were crucial components for making batteries to power electric cars, trucks, and supply power grids, as well as to support the New Green Deal initiatives of the world. In exchange for exclusive mining rights, Hexitron investors agreed to split the profits with the Moldovia government. Alexander persuaded the President of Moldovia, Sergio Kaminski, to nationalize all natural resources in the country, securing Hexitron's dominance in the market. However, Alexander kept his partnership with Hexitron a secret, and his wealth was concealed in a Swiss bank account. Moldovia became one of the wealthiest and most powerful nations in the world, Hexitron a multinational corporation generating vast profits, and Alexander a rising star, gaining popularity not only in Moldovia but in the entire Global World Government (GWG).

Rumors spread that Alexander may have poisoned President Kaminski, but no one dared to speak up, fearing the wrath of Alexander and his powerful allies. The batteries produced by Hexitron were hailed as cleaner and less polluting than fossil fuels by the GWG, and Alexander manipulated this hysteria of global warming to persuade the governments of the United States and Europe to switch to battery-powered energy. While Russia and China claimed to support this movement, they continued to use fossil fuels, remaining the largest polluters on the planet. Alexander used Moldovia's profits to purchase power grids worldwide, regardless of whether they were fossil fuel-driven or electric, as long as they were profitable. Governments worldwide embraced this shift to clean green power, forming alliances to share the costs of becoming green instead of relying on their countries' abundant coal, gas, and oil. However, China and Russia never intended to comply with the agreement.

Alexander's genius lay in his ability to finance his country's military using the money pouring in from the new green movement and other power grid purchases. While the rest of the world focused on establishing a global world government without borders, Alexander built up his military, and nobody noticed his sudden rise to power or his increased military spending.

Meanwhile, Alexander was planning his own world domination plan. Ten years after the disappearance of millions of people, which had led to the collapse of the world economies, Dimitrov's plan could finally be implemented. The timing was perfect, as he had spent the past decade preparing and building his military for his planned takeover. When chaos erupted, Alexander was ready to achieve his goal of a global takeover.

Phase One of his plan involved sending his armies into three weak and easy-to-conquer European countries. It took his military two years to defeat these countries' militaries, crush all resistance, and replace their leadership with his own puppet administration. He then repaired their power grids and communications networks. Once this was accomplished, he initiated Phase Two of his plan by promising six other former European Union countries, who had joined the GWG until it collapsed, that he would replace their power grids and not invade their countries if they joined his New World Order government. Since these six nations were in shambles and needed stability, they agreed to join Alexander's New World Order in return for his promise to get their power grids and communication systems running and provide needed food supplies. This avoided a war with Moldovia and created a powerful ten-nation government with Alexander as its leader.

Phase Three of Alexander's plan began after he had all ten countries in his new union stabilized, with their power and cyber networks running efficiently. With this accomplished, he promised to rebuild the rest of the world's power grids, communications, and cyber networks if they joined his New World Order. He also promised to create stability, re-establish a global banking and monetary system enforce order, and bring peace and unification to the global community. He promised every country that joined their movement that their social media would be restored. Alexander gave a powerful message to what was left of any world leaders and its citizens crying out "I promise I will bring you Peace, Prosperity,

Global Stability and Order. I will put food in your stomachs and clothes on your children!"

However, what Almeria did not know, but had been revealed to a small group of witnesses by Elijah before he started preaching on the Jerusalem steps, was that Alexander Dimitrov had made a pact with the Dark Lord from the spiritual world. He had been given power by powers and principalities to rule the world with the Dragon, who is also known as the Dark Lord, whose real name is Satan. Satan had an army of fallen angels prepared to do battle on the side of Alexander and his earthly army. The Dragon would enter the Supreme Leader, who had been brought out of a coma, and was permitted by God to reign for seven years before Jesus would come back with his army of believers to defeat him. God was allowing this as he would bring Judgment against wicked people who not only hated him but had sold themselves to the Antichrist (Beast), and his Un-Holy Prophet (Little Beast). These rebellious people could be recognized by 'The Mark' they received on their forehead or right hand by declaring and worshiping the Supreme Leader as God. God also wanted to give one last chance to the people of the world, who had not yet received 'The Mark', to repent and receive salvation.

Almeria recounted how she had seen Alexander Dimitrov morph from a supposedly compassionate young man into a cunning politician who schemed his way into the most powerful position in Moldovia through deceit and falsehoods. With the help of his influential parents, he used their political and corporate connections to ascend to the top of the global power structure. Almeria found it absurd when Alexander claimed to be a deity, as it was far beyond her comprehension. This was the tipping point for her conversion to Christianity. She resolved never to succumb to the Mark of the Beast, regardless of the consequences. Upon hearing the Two Witnesses preach that Jesus was God's Son and had died for her sins, Almeria gave her heart to God. She repented, invited Christ into her life, and became a valiant fighter in God's army.

Chapter 20

Jamil & Hua Lee join the Fight

After learning about the Supreme Leader's secret pact with
the Dark Lord, two more people joined our group. Their names
were Jamil and Hua Lee, and they overheard Almeria and me
discussing our witness efforts at our hidden camp in the mountains
near Jerusalem. Jamil and Hua Lee asked if they could join us in
our plan to risk death and travel to small towns throughout Israel
and surrounding countries to share the gospel message and warn
people never to receive 'The Mark.'

The four of us were Christians saved by faith: Jamil, an ex-
Muslim from Africa; Almeria, from the European country of
Moldovia; Hua Lee, from China; and me, a refugee from the once-
powerful United States. Since my family were believers who had
been raptured, I felt that God was leading me to return to the small
towns outside Israel to practice preaching, with the eventual goal of
returning to America. Each of my new friends had similar plans.
Jamil intended to witness with us but warned that he had a burden
to return to Africa as soon as possible to preach the gospel to the
Muslim people. Almeria felt inspired by the Holy Spirit to help us
witness in Israel, with her ultimate goal being to return to Moldovia

and share God's message there. Hua Lee felt called to return to China and witness there.

Despite the danger of being hunted by the New World Order, we continued preaching the Gospel throughout Israel and its neighboring countries. Our success was beyond our expectations, as people who had witnessed the destruction caused by the New World Order accepted Jesus as their Messiah in great numbers.

However, the Lord placed an increasing burden on our hearts to return to our homelands to preach the Gospel, even though we had no NWO passports, means of transportation, or money since we refused 'The Mark.' We made the decision to return home and locked hands, knelt down, and asked God for direction on how to get there. The Holy Spirit spoke the same words to each of us, "Believe that it is possible, and it will happen." We responded, "All things are possible for God, so yes, we believe!" Miraculously, we found ourselves in our homelands. I was back in what we used to call America, and I knew my friends were in their own countries as well.

Chapter 21

Sarah Back Home- How the USA Ceased to Exist

Now that I am back in my home country, once called the United States, I feel the need to provide a more detailed history lesson of how America ceased to exist. Please forgive me if I repeat information I have already covered, but I believe a deeper analysis of the fall of the USA is critical to understanding why I had to return to preach to its former citizens.

As I mentioned previously, a secret society or deep state of powerful corporate and past government leaders, who were liberal socialists, desired global power at any cost. They used their influence to manipulate both sides of the political parties by funding their political campaigns through corporate lobbyists. Whenever a politician or even a President became too powerful, they used every means possible to crush any dissent to their globalist ambitions. They set up entrapments, impeachment proceedings, and lies to discredit and destroy any conservative patriotic leaders. When these tactics failed, they found ways to manipulate elections in their favor. They even paid anarchists to infiltrate political rallies to cause mayhem and disputes. Any conservative nationalistic movement was quickly suppressed by the deep state-controlled media, which continually gave it negative publicity. Eventually, this led to the formation of a world governing body called the Global World Government (GWG). The deep state leaders manipulated the United States government leadership to help create the GWG. In order to accomplish this, the United States of America would give up its sovereignty and agree to be ruled by this new global government.

The deep state leaders then agreed to enrich the leadership of most of the world governments if they would convince their people that it was in their best interests to join the USA in creating the GWG. The majority of countries around the world proceeded to join and be governed by this new world government. The deep state then installed their own puppet chancellor to preside over this new global utopian society. However, Russia and China refused to join the GWG and were ecstatic when the United States, the most powerful nation in the world at the time, disbanded and joined the GWG. Both Russia and China, armed with nuclear weapons and large militaries, saw this as their opportunity to gain more power in their respective corners of the world. Russia became the power in the north, while China became the power in the east. The other countries that refused to join the GWG were Israel and Iran. The deep state leaders were not happy with this refusal, and these countries became their next targets. With money comes power, and that made their global one-world government all the more plausible.

My parents, grandparents, brother, and sister were enraged and started warning everyone that the end of the world predicted by the prophet Daniel was at hand. They claimed the Anti-Christ was soon to be revealed and would take over the world. They begged everyone to repent and accept Jesus Christ as their Lord and Savior. They told me to make the decision quickly, as they knew the rapture of the church was soon to take place. Oh, how I wish I knew then what I know now and believed them. But at that time in my life, I was stubborn and believed in this new utopian society, where everyone would live in common housing communities and share food, shelter, and be equal.

As I have mentioned many times throughout this letter, the world collapsed in one day when millions of people disappeared, including my family. 'All gone' in the blink of an eye. I knew immediately that I had backed the wrong horse and that my family was raptured and now with the Lord in Heaven. What a fool I had been, but now that I am finally saved and a Christian, I must stay and fight.

What happened after all the people disappeared resulted in the total collapse of the Global World Government. The remaining governments of the world, including Iran, Russia, and China, also crumbled. The banking system collapsed, causing widespread panic. The deep state leaders lost billions of dollars, leading many of them to commit suicide. Complete anarchy spread throughout the world as the power grids, which were expensive to maintain, shut down after the foreign governments that had promised abundant mineral supplies for the green movement collapsed. The GWG countries could no longer rely on cheaper fossil fuels as their companies had already shifted to cleaner electricity and battery power. The entire world was in utter chaos, except for Moldovia, a small country that had been planning for this collapse for years under the leadership of Alexander Dimitrov, a little-known leader.

Chapter 22

Sarah & the Militias

Here I was, back at home in what was once the greatest country in the world, now fallen into the shadows of evil. Various militia groups had taken control of different parts of the country. When the Rapture occurred and the World Global Government fell apart in the ensuing chaos, everyone, including corporations backed by the Deep State, lost their money and power. The last vestiges of goodness in this once-proud nation disappeared when Christians were Raptured. Evil ran rampant. A few of us realized that this was the Christian Rapture as mentioned in the Bible, and we finally saw the error of our ways and became Christians. Some of these new Christians realized that they must preach the Gospel.

News was scarce as communication and power grids shut down, and people in colder climates were freezing to death. People flocked to the warmer climates in the South, but food shortages were widespread. Like during the Great Depression, those who lost all their money in the World Bank's collapse committed suicide by the thousands. People were murdering each other over food and shelter, and anarchy and chaos reigned throughout the world.

The only place that seemed to be doing well was the New World Order, led by the vicious and charismatic leader, Alexander Dimitrov. Years before the chaos started, Dimitrov had used his country's wealth and power to build the largest military in the world. He was then able to take over the countries that once made up the Roman Empire.

What was left of the United States of America, which had later become part of the World Global Government, was now splintered into separate militias, each with different leadership called warlords. At this time, Alexander Dimitrov and his newly formed New World Order did not see these former World Global Government countries as a threat. However, years later, after he had solidified his power with the revived Roman Empire countries, Alexander proposed a deal with the leader of the strongest militia, Thomas Martin. Alexander would provide power grids, communications, cyber networks, and food to the militias in return for their agreement to join the New World Order. Thomas Martin sent a message to all the warlord leaders, asking them to meet to discuss the NWO proposal. Many of these warlords agreed to meet, as they were tired of constant fighting among the different militias, and many of their followers were in need of food and supplies.

Alexander then sent the NWO Ambassador, Babel Nero, to meet with the militia leaders to discuss the details of the proposal. Babel emphasized that the warlords and their followers must agree to receive a "Mark" on their foreheads or right hands as a promise of complete mind, body, and spiritual allegiance to the

New World Order and its Supreme Leader, Alexander Dimitrov.

Since most of the people of this once-great nation had supported the move to the World Global Union, it did not seem like a big deal to change alliances to the New World Order. Besides, many were starving, and there seemed to be no end to the chaos. Therefore, the majority of the warlord leaders and their supporters agreed to join the New World Order and started requiring their followers to receive the "Mark."

I found myself in the midst of a transition from the warlord system to the New World Order and sought God's guidance. He led me to a militia that refused to join the New World Order and receive the Mark. After I preached and explained the events that led up to the rise of the NWO to power, many in the group believed in my message to repent, be baptized, and invite Jesus into their hearts. They became new creations in Christ and protected me as I preached the Gospel to anyone who would listen. To my surprise, many others also saw the NWO as an evil empire, and the Holy Spirit convicted them of their need to repent of their sins and commit their lives to Jesus Christ.

The New World Order established key militia leaders and their small armies as peacekeepers to enforce law and order. A federal court system was set up with judges trained in the doctrine of the New World Order, its Prophet, and the Supreme Leader. Babylon became the capital of the NWO, and the Supreme handpicked NWO Ruling Council set policies and global laws that were enforced in the former United States. A global tribunal legal system was also established, with kangaroo courts and judges having absolute authority.

I continued to preach the Gospel for three years, witnessing the power of God falling from heaven and seeing hundreds of conversions. Although I wasn't trained as a preacher, God gave me the right words to speak to reach the hearts of those He placed in my path.

Chapter 23

Jamil-Witness to Muslims, Magog's Origins

Before discussing Jamil's witnessing to Muslims in North Africa, a brief history lesson of Northern Africa and the Islamic resurgence is necessary. Northern Africa, which includes Libya, Turkey, Sudan, and Iran, was mostly Muslim and, like many other countries, was in total disarray following the Rapture. At the same time, Russia, which also has a large Muslim population, had fallen into chaos as well. An Islamic leader arose out of the chaos who was from what was left of the ancient Russian Islamic nations. He believed he was called by Allah to be the Caliphate, and his name was Magog. He rallied the people of these former countries into a new world jihadist movement. He created alliances with the terrorist groups that still existed in the Muslim countries of North Africa and Russia. His army grew day by day, and their major theme, as it was in the past, was to destroy Israel and create a worldwide Islamic State. Many of these people rallied around Magog and believed he was the new prophet and the Caliphate. Their armies poured in from all the former Islamic nations, and soon they had over a million heavily armed and trained militia. Magog had his spies throughout these lands, and whenever someone opposed his rule in these former Middle Eastern and

African territories, these blasphemers were brought in chains before him and beheaded. Magog, the self-declared Caliphate, made all his army swear allegiance to Allah. He hated Israel with a passion and used the treaty that the New World Order had made with Israel to rally his Muslim followers to form a great army to move against the New World Order and Israel. They marched towards Israel.

Before his march, Magog had been invited by the Supreme Leader of the New World Order to join him, being promised power and authority over all the North. He had originally agreed to consider this proposal (in order to stall long enough to fortify and enlarge his military) but kept making excuses, prolonging this merger. In his heart, Magog wanted nothing to do with this infidel leader and his False Prophet. He led his army against the New World Order and Israel, and as explained earlier, they were defeated after a great earthquake occurred just outside of Jerusalem and swallowed up much of his army. Magog's plans of dominating the world were destroyed, and he was killed in this battle.

Jamil had originally been part of Magog's army and had followed Magog into battle against Israel and the New World Order. Finding himself just outside of Jerusalem after the battle was lost, Jamil had escaped to the mountains after barely surviving the earthquake and fire from heaven that had devastated most of Magog's warriors. Jamil would have most certainly been put to death if found by the NWO troops. Why he was spared when so many of his military brothers were killed, he could not explain.

Before meeting Jamil in the mountains surrounding Jerusalem, he had told me that he was a fanatical follower of Allah and his prophet Mohammed. However, after his escape from the Battle of Magog against Israel and the New World Order, he felt very depressed and had a dream that was so vivid that he knew it was from God. In the dream, a great peace came over him, and Jesus appeared to him and spoke, "I am God's Son, and I am The Way, The Truth, and The Life. Jamil, I died and rose again so that you may have eternal life. You must repent of your sins and follow me. I have left a Bible for you in your secret hiding place, and when you wake up, retrieve it, study it, and if you believe, give your life to me." The next day, Jamil found the Bible in his secret hiding place, known only to him. He read it every day for a month and soon became a believer in Christ. He repented of his sins and gave his life to Christ.

Jamil, who was now a Christian, preached the gospel with us to hundreds of people in the region around Jerusalem. He preached to anyone who would listen to his testimony, stating, "Friends, I was a dedicated Muslim, believing in the Koran, Prophet Mohammed, and Allah, but Jesus came to me in a dream and changed everything. He is a prophet in the Koran, but he revealed to me in a dream that he is God's only Son. He opened my eyes to the truth, and I now believe the Bible verse John 3:16, which states, 'For God so loved the world that he gave his one and only Son, that whoever believes in him shall not perish but have eternal life.' That Son is Jesus Christ, who died for our sins in order that we might receive salvation. Believe, repent of your sins, ask him to come into your heart, and he will." Many of the people he preached to came to Christ as the Holy Spirit had been convicting them and drawing them to the real Messiah.

However, Jamil had a longing to go back to Northern Africa and preach to the Muslim people. After preaching with our team around Jerusalem for several years, the Holy Spirit placed Jamil back in Northern Africa, where his testimony brought thousands of Muslims to Christ.

Chapter 24

Hua Lee- Witness to China,

Zang Wei- Origins

Hua Lee had returned to China and witnessed the aftermath of the Rapture on her former nation. The disappearance of millions of Chinese who had covertly converted to Christianity through underground churches had caused chaos that the communist government could not explain. The world financial collapse had stripped the government's highest officials of their wealth, leaving them unable to address the angry citizens who demanded answers. The resulting riots and anarchy had spread throughout major cities, until a strong military general named Zhang Wei organized enough troops loyal to him to quell the rebellion. Military tribunals were established to eliminate any threats to his military dictatorship, resulting in the execution of former communist government officials and the disappearance of rebellion leaders and sympathizers.

Hua Lee had preached the Gospel with us for several years in Jerusalem, and after asking God to send her back to her home country, she found herself preaching in China. Everywhere she went, people hungered for God, and thousands gave their lives to Christ. With no communication networks working and news scarce, many Chinese were starving and living day to day. Hua Lee was joined by some members of the 144,000 Jewish Christians in China to spread the Gospel, and many citizens who had been denied knowledge of Christ by the former communist government now converted to Christianity. Only the military and its leaders refused to believe, and after ten years, they rebuilt their military to become one of the largest in the world.

Zhang Wei and his generals had initially refused to become part of the New World Order, but after many years of negotiation, they made a pact with the Supreme Leader. In exchange for assistance in rebuilding China's infrastructure, including communication networks and the power grid, the New World Order demanded that China use its military to destroy the Israeli extremists hiding in mountain caves and raiding throughout the territories of the New World Order. This provided a great opportunity for Zhang and his generals to test their weapons and military might on the Israeli army, which was no match for China's superior two million-person army. Zhang was quoted by one of his generals as saying, "We will destroy Israel first and then turn our war machine on the New World Order armies."

Zhang Wei suspected that it was Alexander Dimitrov who had started the cyber war against China, which had shut down all communications in the country after the disappearance of millions of Chinese citizens. This breakdown had resulted in the fall of the communist government. Zhang knew that the Chinese communist government had originally plotted to destroy all the nations of the world through Artificial Intelligence (AI), but they failed. AI was computerized software intelligence that could solve problems and provide information on anything the user was utilizing, including cell phones, internet correspondence, and military and corporate secrets. Chinese intelligence officers were using this technology to spy on people all over the world, track their movements, and eavesdrop on them in their own homes through televisions, cell phones, and computers.

Zhang was convinced that Alexander Dimitrov had used similar technology, set up through Hexitron, to destroy the entire world's cyber network, including that of China. Now, nations whose citizens were under the control of the New World Order were forcing their people to receive a Mark of allegiance on their foreheads or right hands. Zhang believed that this was a sly way to monitor their citizens' actions by embedding a computer chip in each Mark. He suspected that the Mark was connected to a supercomputer that could track and record everything each person was doing at all times, effectively controlling their lives.

Zhang Wei vowed never to let his people receive the Mark and bow down to Alexander. He had learned from the communist leadership that there were no gods, only man, and Alexander was no god.

Chapter 25

The Cyber Wars-Origins

As I, Sarah Rebecca, await my imminent appearance before the New World Orders kangaroo court Judge, who was selected by the Prophet of the New World Order, I realize that her time is short and expect to be found guilty of sedition. In anticipation of this, I want to educate my readers about another ploy that Alexander used to rise to power and eventually control most of the world. As I previously mentioned in her document, the Cyber Wars began a few days after the chaos caused by the disappearance of millions of people all over the world, which was later called the Rapture. The sudden disappearance of millions of Christians caused panic, with planes and cars crashing due to the sudden absence of pilots and drivers. The United States was no longer in existence and had become part of the Global World Government (GWG).

Many people throughout the GWG who believed in the green movement blamed the disappearance on atmospheric conditions caused by climate change, while anarchists bent on forcing the GWG to disband and go back to separate countries claimed that the government kidnapped and killed people who disagreed with their policies. Some people even believed that Russia and China, who refused to join the global movement, were responsible for the chaos and anarchy that ensued as a result of this disappearance.

Shortly after the Rapture, a Cyber War began between the GWG, Russia, China, and Moldovia. They all tried to take advantage of the chaos to destroy each other's cyber networks, power grids, and communications, with the winner of the cyber war being Moldovia. Moldovia's leader, Alexander, had a plan in operation for many years before the Rapture took place to take over the GWG, Russia, and China and make a new world empire with himself in control. Moldovia used the Hexitron Corporation Cyber scientists and professional hackers to systematically destroy all the power grids, communication networks, and computer systems of all the nations of the world. Their AI software was designed to jump from computer system to computer system throughout the globe and turn each cyber system against itself, leaving Moldovia as the only country with operational cyber computers.

Moldovia's success in the Cyber War was due to their advanced knowledge of a prophesied world collapse that was communicated to them by witches and spiritualists, which Alexander used to prepare his Hexitron cyber scientists and professional hackers years in advance. Alexander also sent out paid anarchists into cities throughout the world to start riots once chaos started. The Dark Lord also gave Alexander the idea to build a strong military and have them ready to send them against the weakest nations of the former European Union once the chaos started. The military was built over ten years of planning, preparation, and implementation.

As soon as the rapture happened, Dimitrov knew it was time to launch his plans for world domination. He bided his time until the Global World Government, the World Bank, and the remaining governments of China and Russia began to crumble. After winning the Cyber War, he ordered his paid anarchists, who were strategically placed in major cities around the world, to incite riots. They were instructed to destroy any remaining power and communication stations that had not yet been destroyed by the Artificial Intelligence.

As a result of this cyber terrorism, power grids were sabotaged, and communication networks were destroyed. Those living in colder climates were left without heat, causing some to freeze to death. Meanwhile, those in warmer climates were unable to refrigerate their food, causing it to rot and leading to starvation. People could no longer rely on their televisions, radios, social media, or computers as they had all been destroyed. Cities were exploding with riots, and people were panicking from fear of being next to disappear, encouraged by Alexander's paid anarchist.

The governments of powerful nations like the Global World Government, China, and Russia soon failed without their power, communications, and computers.

Chapter 26

The War to End All Wars

Alexander professed to desire peace for all people, but in reality, his goal was to dominate the entire planet. He possessed the world's most sophisticated weaponry, thanks to his artificial intelligence, which enabled his military to render all atomic missiles controlled by other countries' computers inoperable. He had assembled a million-person army trained by the world's top military officers, recruited from major special forces.

As the Supreme Leader of the NWO, Alexander had taken control of the original Roman Empire countries, then coerced and manipulated former Global World Government countries to join the New World Order government. He had even made a deal with former warlords from the USA, who agreed to force their people to receive the Mark. Now he waited for the right time to break his alliance with China once they had finished suppressing resistance forces in the mountains around Israel.

To secure China's military support, Alexander extended an olive branch to a Chinese military general named Zang Wei, who had taken over China after the fall of the Communist regime. The rapture of many Chinese Christians had caused rioting in major cities, and the Cyber Wars had caused all communications and power to be lost, leading to citizens' revolt. Alexander promised to help restore China's communications, power grids, and food supplies, and in return, China would make its multi-million-person military available to the NWO when needed. General Zang agreed, not because he believed it was in China's best interest, but because he needed the restoration of his cyber network, communications, and power grids to maintain power in the most populous nation on earth. He suspected that Moldovia, led by Alexander, had destroyed China's power grids and communication systems during the Cyber Wars. While General Zang would not forget Alexander's treachery, he would bide his time until the right moment to strike back.

Russia was not a significant threat to Alexander and the New World Order, as they had already been in financial trouble before the rapture and had lost many of their Muslim populations in their defeat to the NWO outside of Jerusalem. Alexander's spies had informed him that Russia's nuclear weapons had been rendered obsolete when Alexander's scientists destroyed their computer systems. The destruction of Russia's authoritarian government and the death of their president, Michal Vladimir, had left the country in a third-world state, according to Alexander's spies.

Israel had been neutralized after the first war, as they had lost over half of their army fighting Magog. Alexander had tried to exterminate the Jewish army but failed, as many of their troops broke through the lines of NWO troops and fled to the mountains, where they built an almost impenetrable stronghold of interconnected caves. These caves formed a natural barrier that protected the Jews from aerial attack, and the only way to approach them would be to scale high cliffs. Alexander's plan was to use China's military to break through and destroy the remaining Israel army, which would be a difficult task and cost many Chinese troops.

Alexander's spies had informed him that China was in the process of assembling a massive military comparable to his own NWO one. China had made strides toward rebuilding its military after the communist regime imploded due to the chaos of losing millions of its citizens. A military leader named Zang Wei had gathered a few faithful military generals who helped him form a military dictatorship. But Alexander knew that what Zang needed desperately was to restore power, food, and communications in order to maintain his fist hold on the Chinese people. Failure to do this would bring another uprising of the people. Therefore, Alexander made a peace proposal with Zang and his generals to restore power, communications, and provide much-needed food to China in exchange for the use of their military in weeding out the Israelis from their caves in Jordan.

The deal was made, and after three and a half years, Alexander lived up to his promise and provided Zang with his needed network of food, power, and communications to be hooked up to the New World Order Network. As per their agreement, Zang marched his armies toward Jerusalem and the mountains of Jordan to fulfill his half of the bargain made with Alexander. After all, China always hated Israel, and this gave them an excuse to utterly destroy Israel once and for all. However, Zang and his war machine had been rebuilt to be a global powerhouse.

So, after he took care of helping Alexander defeat Israel, his generals would then march on Babylon, Alexander's capital, and annihilate the New World Order and its fake god.

Zang Wei believed he was a descendant of Genghis Khan, the fiercest empire warrior the world has ever known, and led his two million-person army across the Euphrates River on its journey toward Israel. Zang was astonished that the great Euphrates River was completely dried up. This made his army's passage to Israel relatively easy. When he arrived at the mountains surrounding Israel, called Petra, he prepared his force for battle. Alexander had informed him this would be a fairly easy battle to win, as the Israelites that escaped the battle of Magog were depleted and would not be able to put up much of a fight. However, the opposite was true, as the Israelis were a fiercely trained and battle-tested group of warriors. Rooting them out of their mountain strongholds would soon prove to be a difficult task and would be costly in the loss of life. The Chinese army was repelled time after time, often retreating to secure ground. The battle lasted for many weeks, with the Chinese taking heavy losses. The Chinese continually advanced toward the Israelites with their missiles, guns, and attack helicopters but kept being repelled as the Israelis were well fortified and had to be rooted out with hand-to-hand combat.

Alexander knew that the Israelis had rebuilt their army and fortifications over the past three and a half years since he had entered the temple and desecrated it. He had also killed their prime minister. For this reason, Israel would be ready to defend themselves down to the last person, and there would be massive bloodshed. China would lose a large part of their forces, weakening them and making them vulnerable to a devastating blow from Alexander's world armies. Alexander told his generals, "They think they are my allies, but they are the final threat to my world domination and will not be expecting us to come against them. I will also use Israel's nuclear weapons against China if things go wrong." The only nuclear weapons left after the Cyber Wars were Israel's and the New World Order's. Alexander, now filled with the Dark Lord's spirit, would soon destroy the last threat to his kingdom: the massive Chinese military and its leader, Zang Wei.

The field of Armageddon was filled with blood, as were the mountains and valleys in Jordan. Alexander could not wait any longer for the Chinese to destroy Israel, as it was taking too long. He moved his army against the Chinese military, who had lost over half their forces to the Israeli army. In the fierce fighting, the Chinese leader, Zang Wei, was killed. Those that remained of the Chinese army were then surrounded by the New World Order armies, and without Zang Wei's leadership, they surrendered. These remaining Chinese troops were then given a choice: receive the Mark and join the New World Order or be killed. Most chose to receive the Mark and pledge their allegiance to the NWO. However, many others refused the Mark, having remembered Hua Lee's Gospel message and asked Christ into their hearts. When they refused the Mark, they were murdered by the NWO troops.

Alexander's war machine was even larger with the addition of the Chinese force. Israel had no chance of withstanding such a multitude of troops and war machines.

Chapter 27

The Judgments and Trials

Jamil's Final Testimony

So, here we are on trial for sedition against the New World Order: Jamil in Africa, Hua Lee in China, Almeria in what was once Europe, and I in the former USA. Jamil was somehow able to send me a text message typing, "Sarah, be strong in Christ for our redemption draws close. I feel the presence of the Holy Spirit more than I ever have in my life. Jesus is my best friend and has promised us a great reward. My only regret is that I could not be present with Hua Lee, Almeria, and you. My friends have shared the news that the Two Witnesses who had brought down hellfire and plagues on the people who received the 'Mark of the Beast' as judgment are now dead. During their time here on earth, they brought down from heaven great judgment from God upon the Mark blasphemers by scorching them with fire, giving them horrific plagues, and causing painful sores to cover their bodies. My friends said they personally witnessed on NWO Cable News the people who received the Mark and did not die from these judgments dancing in the streets, singing, and crying out joyfully that the two Witnesses and their God are dead! My friends said they had never seen such horrible judgment that God rained down on those people who had received the Mark. Instead of repenting and turning to God, they hated God even more.

I have just been called before the tribunal, and my time is short. Pray for me that I will have the courage to stand for my Lord and Savior Jesus Christ and share his gospel. See you on the other side!"

That was the last I heard from Jamil, but word got back to me from a Christian witness who said Jamil was taken away and beheaded with no trial. He said that before Jamil died, his face shone like that of an angel (like Stephen in the Bible before he was stoned to death) as he was witnessing to his fellow Muslims even as they lifted the ax.

Word also got back to me that Hua Lee was given the opportunity to preach to the Chinese military generals before they left to assist Alexander in their quest to defeat the Israelites who had fled to the mountains around Petra, in Jordan. They did this in response to Alexander's decree to exterminate the entire Jewish population and anyone who had joined the resistance. Hua Lee was brought before China's General Zang in chains, and she proceeded to share the gospel with Zang and his men. Zang declared, "Hua Lee, you have almost persuaded me to become a Christian." He commanded, "Release Hua Lee as she has done no wrong." Many of those who had heard her testimony gave their lives to Christ then and there. Zang then announced, "Hua Lee, I promise to return to China triumphantly and listen to you more, after I destroy

Israel. I also promise my men that I will bring back the head of Alexander, after I turn on him and destroy his army." The cheers of Zang's army personnel cried out, "Death to Alexander and his false prophet!"

After I read Jamil's letter to my cellmate and shared with her Hua Lee's witness in China, she burst into tears and gave her heart to the Lord. Several other inmates who were incarcerated with me also accepted Christ that day after I shared my testimony with them. Later that day, I received news that my trial had been moved up, and I was to face the New World Order Judge the next day. I was filled with fear, but that night, Jesus appeared to me in a vision while I was in bed. His supernatural love overwhelmed me, and he placed his hand on my shoulder, telling me to be strong and that he would soon take me home. He explained that he needed me to go before some very powerful people and give my last testimony.

Chapter 28

My Trial and Judgment, Sarah

I prayed all night, knowing my trial was the next day, and I was filled with the Spirit of the Living God. Jesus came to me in a vision and spoke to me, telling me to be strong and have courage.

The next morning, armed guards led me in chains to the chambers of the New World Order Judge. I was forced down on my knees as the sheriff knocked my legs out from under me. Prostrate on the ground, I was expected by the crowd of NWO reporters to beg for my life. The bailiff cried out, "All people in this courtroom, bow down before His Honor, the Judge of the mighty New World Order." I stood up, trying to say, "I do not bow down to anyone except my Lord and Savior Jesus Christ," but the Judge immediately told me that I was in contempt of court and to shut up and be seated!

The prosecutor had a wicked gleam in his eye and proceeded to bring the charges laid against me. "Your Honorable Judge, this young lady who stands before you is a cancer to our future Utopian Global Society. Sarah Rebecca has been preaching throughout the land for the past seven years that there is only one God, who exists as the Father, Son, and Holy Ghost. She is aware that this doctrine has been outlawed for many years, yet she still preaches this Gospel boldly and confidently to all who will listen. She also claims to be a Christian, and everyone knows this doctrine and its false leader, Jesus Christ, are against the law. She refuses to receive the 'Mark' and tells her followers it is Satanic, and anyone who receives this Mark will have to face God's judgment in the afterlife. She refuses to bow down and submit to the authority of the One World Religion, the Supreme Leader, and the Prophet. She carries an outlawed book called the Bible. All these things are against our societal beliefs, and this sedition demands the death penalty."

My defense lawyer jumped out of his chair and stated that, yes, his client is a believer in Jesus Christ and is a Christian. "This is not her fault, Your Honor, as I believe she has been led astray by the two Witnesses and their followers that preached and taught this ancient religion and philosophy. She truly believes that this Jesus is the only way to God, and that nobody can be saved but through him. I ask the court to have mercy upon her and allow her to be sentenced to a re-education camp. There she can be indoctrinated in the understanding that the Supreme Leader only wants the best for us, and since he has been transformed before our very eyes from a man into a God, he can open her eyes. She is truly a good person; however, she has been deceived by these Holy Roller Blasphemers. She still believes strongly that the United States of America should never have been disbanded, not realizing that the goal of the New World Order is to create a utopian global society. We are so close to controlling the entire world system now that the

Two Witnesses have left us and their so-called Judgments have ceased. Your Honor, please have mercy."

The Judge spoke up and said, "Let me hear what she has to say for herself, Sarah. Before you speak, know that I have the ability to send you to a re-education camp or sentence you to death for your heresy and sedition against the New World Order. You seem like an intelligent person, and what you say now can make the difference between life or death. Also, if you agree to receive the 'Mark,' reject your Christian beliefs, forfeit your Bible, and bow down to the Supreme Leader and the Prophet, then I can release you."

The crowd in the courtroom and the television audience, as this was broadcast on the NWO News, all let out a huge sigh, and some even rejoiced and proclaimed the Judge to be very merciful. Many were hopeful that Sarah would take the deal, but most hated her because of her faith and hoped she would receive the death sentence.

Sarah rose after praying a silent prayer to the Lord, asking him to anoint her with his power and give her the words to boldly and confidently declare, "Your honor and citizens of the New World Order, your offer to free me in return for me taking the 'Mark', denying my Lord and Savior, and giving you my Bible, but I must respectfully decline. I love God with all my heart, mind, and spirit, and to deny him would mean denying the God who created the entire universe, his forgiving Son Jesus Christ, who died on a cross for my sins, and the Holy Ghost who now lives in and through me. I believe that the Mark of the Beast, as warned by John the Apostle in Revelations in the Bible, would mean I would forfeit eternal life with him. I believe the Supreme Leader is the Antichrist, the Beast of Revelations, and is filled with Satan who gives him his power. The Prophet is a false Prophet who, by his own admission, worships the Dark Lord. For these reasons, I cannot now or ever bow down before the Supreme Leader, his Prophet, or the New World Order. I ask everyone who is listening and has not yet received the Mark of the Beast, the number 666, on their forehead or right hand, to reject this Mark, the Beast, and all the evil associated with the New World Order. If you receive this Mark, you are doomed and will face judgment before God. Please, before it is too late, repent of your sins and receive God's Holy Son Jesus as your Lord and Savior. The Holy Spirit will come into your heart and make you a new person."

As Sarah's speech ended, the courtroom personnel erupted with anger and gnashed their teeth. The prosecutor screamed out, "This is blasphemy!" The countenance of the judge's face visibly turned to that of a wild beast as he declared Sarah guilty as charged and commanded her to be put to death immediately.

As Sarah's remarks were broadcast over the NWO News Network to millions of viewers throughout the world, many people who had not yet received the 'Mark' actually believed Sarah and gave their lives to Christ. Others shook their fists at their TVs or iPhones. Sarah, filled with the Holy Ghost and shining like an angel, bravely walked with her head held high to the execution chamber. Her guards were amazed at the joy and supernatural peace she had as she walked in chains toward her death.

Her martyred death soon spread throughout the global kingdom, and many more people came to salvation because of her bravery and testimony. She was beheaded that day and awoke to find herself in the most beautiful place she had ever seen and in the presence of her family and friends who had been raptured or had died before her. Oh, wow, it was a fantastic reunion! Jesus welcomed her also and exclaimed, "Well done, you faithful servant!"

Chapter 29

The Final Battle

Alexander now set his sights on the remaining Israelites, who were severely weakened by the Chinese army and vastly outnumbered by the NWO war machine. This would be Alexander's final and greatest conquest, making him the "King of the World." After defeating Israel and the resistance forces, there would be no one left to stop his world domination. Empowered and filled with evil, he rode a chariot pulled by eight pure black Arabian horses (befitting a conquering king) and parked it within view of the battlefield but outside of artillery range.

Suddenly, a miracle happened without warning. An army descended from the heavens, made up of all the Christians who had died and gone to heaven. They were led by a man who shone with the brightness of the sun and rode on a white horse - Jesus. Sarah, her parents, grandparents, brother, and sister were among the warriors. They quickly devastated the NWO armies and captured the Supreme Leader, Alexander the Beast, Abaddon, the little Beast, and the fallen angels.

After being soundly defeated, what remained of the NWO armies fell to their knees and confessed that Jesus Christ is Lord. They realized that he was the King of Kings and Lord of Lords, and they had made a horrific mistake by receiving the Mark, which could not be taken back. All the followers of Jesus Christ, the true King of Kings, were given individual crowns, which were then thrown down at Jesus' feet.

For those who had received the Mark of the Beast, they suddenly found themselves before the throne of God with no chance of redemption. Their leader, once called Alexander, was revealed to be the Antichrist, the Beast, and the Prophet Abaddon was revealed to be the "Little Beast" described by John the Apostle in Revelation found in the Bible. From the body of Alexander, the Antichrist, Satan himself emerged and was placed in chains by God's most powerful angels, along with the legion of fallen evil demons that came from the body of the Prophet Abaddon. Both Satan and the demons were thrown into the bottomless pit.

ABOUT THE AUTHOR

Dr. John Timothy (Ed.D. the University of Akron) is an emeritus administrator, coach and professor from Baldwin Wallace University. He also served as a professor and administrator at Cleveland State University and Wittenberg University as well as an administrator at Youngstown State University.

His passion for teaching the Bible has led him to helm junior and senior high, college, career, and adult Bible studies. He has authored and published numerous professional journal articles and several books.

He is an outdoor enthusiast who enjoys: scuba diving, bicycling, hunting, fishing and golfing. He and his wife have two children and five grandchildren and resides in Cleveland, Ohio.